LETTER TO READER

BURY ME WITH THE BUTTERFLIES, is my husband, Scott Stevenson's, third book. His first book, *LOOKS EASY ENOUGH: A JOYFUL MEMOIR OF OVERCOMING DISEASE, DIVORCE, AND DISASTER,* is a memoir about how we survived during a three year period; cancer, divorce, losing our house in a forest fire, and losing our retirement money in a stock market crash. His second book, *DON'T FORGET TO SMELL THE . . . SAWDUST: A CONTRACTOR'S TALE OF SUPPORTING HIS WIFE THROUGH CANCER*, is a memoir of my journey through cancer with support from my husband, Scott. Even though the books have won a few awards, neither has landed on any bestseller lists.

For my husband's third book, *BURY ME WITH THE BUTTERFLIES*, he tried something different. To see what people were reading, he *Googled* the top ten bestselling books over the last ten years. Towards the top of the list was a love story. My husband thought to himself . . . *I know this book - a romance from the past retold in the present . . . I believe I've got a love story in me.* Another book on the top ten list was a mystery based on ancient clues hidden in religious artifacts. Again my husband was familiar with the book and said to himself . . . *a mystery based on old clues hidden in plain sight. I think I can also do that.* My husband had just seen a movie based on ROMEO AND JULIET and thought, *why not have the families of the two lovers at odds with each other.* And finally, he remembered the first rule of writing – write about what you know. S-o-o-o . . . my husband based the lead female of the story on me (he thinks he knows me . . . ha!) and on what he calls my little personality quirks. Her name is Susan Cambell – my name is Susan and Cambell is a play on the name Capulet. The male lead is Scott Montgomery, an architect living in Sedona, Arizona. Yes, my husband's name is Scott, he is an architect, Sedona is one of our favorite places, and Montgomery is a play on the name Montague.

And there you have it, my husband's latest book, *BURY ME WITH THE BUTTERFLIES*. Amanda, an ER nurse, and Mathew, a sculptor, married for ten years, are tired of the big city and ready for the simpler ways of small town living. On a trip through Sedona, Arizona, they stop to check out an abandoned, run down, fifty-year-old house located in a remote, hidden valley that had caught Mathew's imagination while searching for houses online. While exploring the house, Mathew discovers a manuscript in a hidden compartment of a hand carved desk – mysteriously the only piece of furniture in the house. Intrigued by the cover sheet - a picture of a small butterfly with the handwritten words, "1986 – A FEW DAYS BEFORE MY DEATH," Mathew and Amanda settle down on the dusty floor, lean back against the wall, and begin to read. The manuscript tells of the romance between Scott Montgomery – the property's former owner – and Susan Cambell, who first met in 1944 at the age of eight. Mathew and Amanda discover that the manuscript is but the first of several parts hidden throughout Sedona. Clues from the previous installment lead to the next. While purchasing and settling into their Sedona home, Mathew and Amanda work their way through the clues uncovering the mysterious wonders lying just below the beauty of the red rock canyons. With the discovery of each new portion of the story, Mathew and Amanda learn of Scott's and Susan's growing relationship and in the process Amanda and Mathew reaffirm their own love.

Wishing you the best of everything.

Susan Stevenson
Wife of the author, Scott Stevenson

www.burymewiththebutterflies.com

scottstevensonbutterflies@gmail.com

Bury Me
With
The Butterflies

A Novel

By
Scott Stevenson

DEADORA PRESS
Julian, California
deadorapress@gmail.com

createspace.com
(Amazon)

This book is a work of fiction. Names, characters, places, and incidents are the product of the author's imagination and are not to be construed as real. Any resemblance to actual events, locations, or persons, living or dead, is coincidental.

ISBN 978-0-9842810-7-7

Library of Congress Control Number: 2017916833

Printed and bound in the United States of America

3 4 5 6 7 8 9 10

Every effort has been made to trace copyright holders, and the publisher will be happy to correct mistakes or omissions in future editions.

Dedication

This book is dedicated to all us late bloomers in life who didn't reach our full stride until we were well into our fifties and then asked ourselves, "Why the heck did it take so long?"

Here's to learning, having fun, and helping others.

For additional information on
BURY ME WITH THE BUTTERFLIES
Please see
www.burymewiththebutterflies.com

For retail sales:
www.createspace.com/pub/l/createspacedirect.do
Create Space Direct Reseller
(Amazon)

Bury Me

With

The Butterflies

The Beginning

I T was magical. Mathew and Amanda had just turned off a paved
road onto a long gravel driveway, weaving its way through hundred
year old pinion pines and majestic oaks. A thunder shower had
passed through a half hour earlier pulling the deep earthy smells of
mother nature from the damp brown grass and the dusty shrubs of late
summer that lined each side of the drive. The rays of the sun, ninety
minutes from dropping below the horizon, bounced off the red
sandstone cliffs tinting the air a misty shade of rose. The low irregular
shaped shadows of the pinions seemed to stretch on forever in a slow
motion dance across the gently rolling contours.

Mathew had been behind the wheel for the last seven hours,
driving straight through from Provo, Utah, visiting Amanda's parents.
It was her mother's fiftieth birthday celebration, and they still had
another seven hours to drive before reaching the comfort of their
home in San Diego. But first their plan was to make a quick pit stop
in Sedona, Arizona.

As Mathew drove, Amanda half-sitting, half-lying in the
reclined seat next to Mathew, was trying to catch up on her sleep. Last
night had been a late night at her mother's birthday party – they talked
football with her brothers, sang happy birthday around a candle
covered cake, danced in the back yard to old phonograph records and
laughed at the new jokes as well as the old ones they'd heard many
times before. In an effort to block out the light and deaden the sounds

of travel, Amanda had her gray cotton sweatshirt doubled over, resting across her eyes, and tucked behind her ears. Mathew heard a soft low snore on each of her exhales.

Mathew's back muscles were stiff, his eyes were tired, and he had to pee, but at that moment this magical place was renewing his energy and he was feeling pretty darn good. Most of all, he was excited because he was very hopeful he'd discover, at the end of this driveway, the answers to his six–month long obsession.

*   *   *

Amanda and Mathew were high school sweethearts born and raised in a small town in southern Utah where everyone knew what everyone else was doing, what they had done yesterday, and what they were planning on doing tomorrow. Growing up in a small town, Amanda and Mathew had done all the things high school sweethearts were supposed to have done – they wore their school colors of green and gold as they cheered for their football team on Friday nights, they picnicked at the river with friends on summer afternoons, roasted hot dogs over bonfires in the winter, attended all the dances and school functions together, did homework together, ate meals with each other's families and talked about everything – they were inseparable. Both received better than decent school grades and neither really got into any serious trouble. While their friends were dating and breaking up, and dating and breaking up, Amanda and Mathew stayed together – they said, "It just felt right."

Mathew and Amanda were married shortly after graduation in a small, one room, red brick Methodist church on the south end of Main Street, surrounded by friends and family. At the end of the service, the church bells were rung, echoing through the town and surrounding countryside, letting the city folk and the rural farmers know that Amanda and Mathew were officially linked. Their parents weren't enthusiastic about their wedding plans, after all they were only eighteen years old at the time, but their parents loved both of them, trusted them, and wished them all the best.

Amanda and Mathew had big plans; she loved helping others, enjoyed being in the middle of the action, and wanted to become an emergency room nurse. Mathew loved creating things – turning ideas into reality. His goal was to become an artist, preferably a sculptor.

Shortly after their wedding, they moved to San Diego, California so that Amanda could attend the *San Diego School of Nursing*, which offered a four-year degree in nursing and an extra year to qualify in emergency room procedures. To pay the bills, Mathew worked as a carpenter for several small construction companies - cutting lumber and hammering nails. And to satisfy his creative urges, on weekends he carved tree trunks into . . . whatever he wanted – mountain lions, eagles, totems. One time he even tried a self-portrait – it wasn't very good and ended up in the firewood box. But it was fun and he learned a few lessons in the process. To Mathew's surprise a few of his carvings were purchased, mostly by friends or by friends of a friend, but what the heck a sale was a sale.

Ten years after their marriage, they lived in a small rented house, built in the late 1950s, just north of downtown San Diego where they had a great view of the city lights and of the ocean beyond. Amanda was an emergency room nurse at *Scripps Hospital* in La Jolla, California. She was a slim, five-foot-four inch, twenty-eight year old, with short blond hair, and the greenest eyes Mathew had ever seen. Mathew believed she was part cat. She ate healthy, watched her weight, and liked to exercise – mostly jog. At times Amanda had a tendency to get frustrated over things she couldn't instantly figure out, which complimented Mathew's easy–going, what's–there–to–get–excited– about attitude. They were both very much in love.

Over the years, Mathew had gradually transitioned from construction into being a full-time sculptor, now working in stone rather than wood. He had entered a few contests, won a few commissions, had a few exhibits in a few art galleries, and people seemed to enjoy his creations. The comment he heard most often was, "It looks so simple," and then a moment later, "But I can't seem to take my eyes off it – I'm mesmerized." Mathew would usually reply with a smile, "Well, I'm just a simple guy from a small town. I don't know complicated." They would typically nod and smile back as they continued to stare transfixed at the sculpture.

Mathew, a little over five-feet-ten inches tall, had thinning brown hair. Amanda liked to tease him by reminding him of how much he looked like his dad, who just happened to be bald (at least Mathew thought she was teasing). Mathew was more into hamburgers and fries than Amanda's salads, but he was physically active. Jogging with Amanda, playing tennis, and chiseling stone was no walk in the park – swinging hammers and using power tools built muscle. And he was very fortunate and appreciative to be doing what he loved. Also it didn't hurt that Mathew had a steady stream of clients that paid him for something he'd happily do for free.

Even though Amanda and Mathew were happy with their lives, they were both getting tired of the city life. The constant noise was driving them batty; the traffic – at times it took ninety minutes to travel ten miles to the hospital; the crowds – there were always crowds of people at the theaters, the restaurants, sporting events, and the beaches; and believe it or not, the dirt – the city was much dirtier than the country what with all the trash, cigarette butts, and dust in the air. Amanda and Mathew were small town people, and they were ready to move back to a simpler way of life.

For the past few months, Mathew had been searching online to see if he could find a small house in a small town that they could use as a weekend getaway and eventually move into full time. About six months ago, he had come across a property in Sedona, Arizona that intrigued him. It was a ten acre parcel with a small group of buildings arranged around a central courtyard. The listing described the main building as having a full kitchen and a living/dining area. All the out structures were said to have restrooms and showers. The property was in need of repair and had been empty for the last ten years.

The listing stated that the value of the property was in its seclusion and privacy, yet still close to the center of town. It also had great views stretching across Sedona and then out into the desert. The listing suggested removing the buildings from the site and starting from scratch – BUILD FROM THE GROUND UP, was displayed in large print across the ad. But what intrigued Mathew the most, were the structures – no way would he demolish them. Mathew pictured Amanda and himself living in the main building and then using the smaller out–buildings just across the courtyard as a bedroom, and another as an office – one for each of them, and another for his studio. When Mathew first saw the photos of the buildings, on the surface all he saw were dilapidated structures covered in overgrown vegetation and broken windows. But there was something about the buildings that had caught his eye, as if he was looking at a raw piece of stone and could see the possibilities of the masterpiece just below the surface.

Over the next few months Mathew researched the property and discovered that the original owner was some sort of builder or designer by the name of Scott Montgomery. The buildings were constructed sometime in the 1950's and were originally used as a *construction learning center.* The information was sketchy, and he couldn't quite figure out what a *construction learning center* was. After Scott Montgomery passed away, the property was bought and sold several times and had been sitting empty and unused ever since. Mathew spent countless hours researching Scott Montgomery, the *construction learning center,* and the history of the property, but found no additional information. He even used *Google Earth* to study the property and the buildings from various angles. Bottom line, he couldn't stop thinking about the place and in Amanda's words he'd become *obsessed* with the property.

Which is why, on their way back to San Diego, they were making a short stop in Sedona to take a quick look at the place. Secretly, Mathew thought Amanda was as intrigued with the property as he was, and he was hoping they'd submit an offer to purchase the property within the next few days. They agreed they wouldn't stay long because they still had a long drive ahead of them, and Mathew had a fast approaching deadline on a sculpture that needed to be completed.

The sculpture was for the atrium of a new restaurant, opening in three and a half months in the upscale community of La Jolla, just north of San Diego. The owners were newlyweds and had named their restaurant, *Togetherness*. They wanted the sculpture to represent, as they said, "The closeness of their relationship, their *togetherness*." Mathew wasn't a hundred percent sure what they had in mind, and he had absolutely no idea what the sculpture was going to look like, but he'd been stumped before and he'd always come up with something . . . eventually.

*   *   *

"Amanda, wake up," Mathew said, as he gently nudged her arm.

Quietly snoring next to him in the front seat of their car, Amanda jerked upright and tried to untangle the sweatshirt from around her head. "What? Where are we? Are we home?" she asked.

"No we're here . . . in Sedona. Look how gorgeous this place is, the pinion pines and the oaks are beautiful." As they rounded the final bend of the driveway, Mathew added, "And look, there's the building."

Throwing her sweatshirt over her shoulder into the back seat, Amanda brought her seat to an upright position. Taking a quick look at the structures, she tentatively said with a hint of disappointment in her voice, "It . . . looks . . . kind of rundown."

Excitedly, Mathew replied, "Yeah it does, but it's been sitting empty for quite some time. And what did you expect? We've seen the pictures online, and we knew it was going to take a little work. The place looks great."

"A little work?" questioned Amanda.

Sitting in the car at the end of the gravel driveway, Mathew leaned forward, resting his arms on the steering wheel, as he stared out through the windshield at the property that had consumed his thoughts for months. His eyes were opened wide with excitement and his lips were parted in awe - he was overwhelmed by what he saw. There were several small low structures with lots of glass and long sloping roofs arranged around a brick-paved courtyard. But it was the main building directly in front of them that had captured Mathew's attention; long and low to the ground with a wide sweeping wood shake roof that in places extended a good fifteen feet beyond the exterior walls. The building was nestled into an outcropping of red sandstone boulders with sandstone brick walls extending out from the roof – forming intimate outdoor spaces. In other areas heavy wood lattice work protruded horizontally from the exterior walls to provide shade for the front windows. At the far end of the building, the lattice merged with the low roof to form a semi-enclosed patio area. In places it was hard to tell the indoor spaces from the outdoor spaces and where the natural red sandstone stopped and the manmade sandstone brick walls began. The entire house was covered in fallen pine needles, crawling vines and wild brush. The paint had long since faded away and a few windows lay open to the elements – their panes of glass sharp and jagged. The main house had literally merged into its natural surroundings.

Still leaning forward on the steering wheel, Mathew turned toward Amanda and with a big smile said, "Wo-o-o-o-o-o isn't it great?"

Turning her head to face Mathew, Amanda half smiled, not nearly as excited as Mathew was, and gently patted him on the shoulder, as she said "Yes, dear."

Turning back to her side of the car, Amanda reached over, opened the car door and took a few slow steps outside – it had been a long ride and she was stiff and tired. Taking in an unhurried deep breath, Amanda stretched her arms high above her head, intertwined her fingers, and slowly bent forward at the waist – her fingers leisurely making their way down to her toes. She then stretched to the right and then to the left. "Oh that feels good," she sighed. Taking in another slow breath she exhaled and turned to look down the valley.

"Will you look at that? What a view!" exclaimed Amanda, her eyes wide as she smiled with a bit more enthusiasm.

The view was mesmerizing. Looking out over the lower valley, they could see the city of Sedona surrounded by sculptured sandstone cliffs. Feathery white clouds glided by while the sun's rays turned the sky and cliffs into every imaginable shade of yellow, pink, and red.

Breaking the stillness of the moment, Amanda abruptly spun towards Mathew, and said, "Okay, let's look at the house. It'll be dark soon, and we need to get back on the road."

Amanda was suddenly all business, remembering that Mathew was behind schedule on the *togetherness* sculpture for the TOGETHERNESS Restaurant in La Jolla and she was concerned that he wasn't going to make the deadline. Mathew, on the other hand, wasn't all that concerned. He'd been behind on other projects and he always seem to finish on time. He'd just as soon spend a little more time admiring this beautiful sunset. But Amanda was right – they had a house to look at.

Following the walkway of red sandstone pavers, Mathew and Amanda headed towards the front door. The porch was shaded by a lattice work of massive crisscrossing timbers covered in wild overgrown vines. The vines hung down through the openings of the lattice and Mathew and Amanda had to push them aside in order to reach the front door – like walking through a jungle of hanging vines.

"What do you think this sign means?" Amanda said, as she pointed at a copper plaque screwed to the header above the entrance door.

Looking up, Mathew focused on the plaque and read aloud, "TO ALL WHO PASS THROUGH THESE DOORS, DO SO WITH A LIGHT HEART IN THE HOPE OF **LEARNING, SHARING,** AND **ENJOYING.**" Looking back at Amanda, Mathew said, "Probably some sort of motto or mission statement. But, I like it." And then to himself Mathew repeated, *"LEARNING - SHARING - ENJOYING."*

Smiling, Amanda added, "Did they have mission statements back in the 1950's?" Glancing Mathew's way, not really expecting him to answer, Amanda took hold of the two handles and with a mighty pull swung the thick heavy wooden doors in their direction. Pushed by the bottom edges of the swinging doors, pine needles and dried leaves scraped along the stone porch. Stepping across the threshold into the oversized entry, Amanda looked around and said, "It's so light in here, as if we're still outside!"

The rays of the sun, filtered by the dusty western windows, reflected off the red sandstone wall opposite the entry doors. The diffused light was the same rose color as the misty sunlight reflecting off the sandstone cliffs outside. "Whoever designed this place knew what they were doing," Mathew said, looking around at the open heavy beams and exposed wood sheathing of the ceiling. "Look how solid the roof and walls are. This place may be a bit dirty and run down, but the basics are all here. A little cosmetic repair and it will be as good as new."

"A little cosmetic repair!" repeated Amanda, lowering her chin and raising her brows. "More like a major renovation." Looking past Mathew, Amanda pointed towards an opening in the far wall and walked through it into what appeared to be the kitchen.

"I'll catch up in a moment," Mathew said in a loud voice, as he headed in the opposite direction towards what he thought was a study or maybe a library. Empty, dusty shelving lined the length of two of the walls and pine needles and oak leaves were scattered around the floor and piled in the corners. A couple panes of glass were broken in the window facing the drive, and he could feel a slight breeze making its way through, rustling the oak leaves on the floor.

Mathew heard Amanda opening and closing cabinets in the kitchen as he walked over to a large desk sitting in the far corner. It was the only furniture in the room. The top was a solid four-inch-thick piece of some kind of wood, maybe walnut, the four legs as big as small tree trunks. Sliding open a drawer, Mathew saw an old rusted paper clip and several dried, cracked rubber bands. In another drawer sat a dust covered clay dog bowl with faded images of flowers lining the top edge. Taking another look at the thick desktop, Mathew thought to himself, "That's a nice piece of wood, I should return someday and salvage it, maybe even use it in one of my sculptures."

Placing both hands under the front lip of the desktop, Mathew bent his knees and lifted. He was hoping it was loose, but, the heavy top didn't budge. Crawling underneath, he tried to figure out how the top was attached to the thick trunk–like legs. Pushing, feeling, and exploring the various parts on the underside of the desk, Mathew came up empty. Realizing that he was going to need some tools and more time than he presently had, Mathew decided to find Amanda and explore the rest of the house while there was still a little daylight left.

Turning and walking towards the kitchen, Mathew suddenly heard a small crash from behind. Startled, he spun around, and saw a small wooden panel lying on the floor beneath the desk. Mathew thought to himself, "I'm pretty sure it wasn't there a moment ago. Maybe I loosened something while exploring the underside of the desk?"

Stepping closer, he saw that the small wooden panel on the floor had slid down from inside the knee space. Down on all fours, Mathew partially maneuvered himself under the desk for a closer look and to see if he could slide the small panel back into place. In the process, he noticed that the fallen panel appeared to have been concealing a thin hidden compartment above the top drawer. Looking closer, he saw that there was some sort of flat package in the hidden space. Curious, he reached in, first making sure there were no spiders lurking around, and pulled out an oilcloth–wrapped package, tied cross ways with two thin pieces of twine. Backing his way out from under the desk, he set the package on top of the desk and slowly pulled the loose ends of the knot securing the twine. Carefully folding back each side of the oilcloth, Mathew uncovered a stack of unlined paper covered in neat hand written text. The paper, yellowed from age, had a few corners missing from what appeared to be hungry insects. At the top of the first sheet of paper, roughly drawn in black ink, was a butterfly. Below the butterfly, in small precise hand writing was:

1986 - A FEW DAYS BEFORE MY DEATH

Hearing a shuffle, Mathew lifted his head and saw Amanda standing in the door way. "The place actually looks quite nice . . . once you get past the dust and spider webs," Amanda remarked, turning her head from side to side as she scanned the room. Noticing that Mathew was looking at something on the desk, she walked over, "What's this?"

"I'm not sure. It looks like someone's diary or story or something." Smiling at Amanda, Mathew continued, "I found it in a secret compartment under the desk."

"A secret compartment?"

"Yeah, no kidding and look at the opening line, '*1986 - A Few Days Before My Death.*'"

"You mean those papers have been here since 1986 and we're the first to read them?" asked Amanda.

"Apparently," Mathew responded with a shrug.

Leaning over Mathew's shoulder, Amanda took a closer look at the stack of papers, and said, "Well, don't just sit there. Read the next page. Let's see what we have."

Amanda and Mathew moved over to the wall with the broken windows. Sitting on the floor, leaning back against the empty bookcases, a ray of sunlight from over their shoulders illuminated the papers as he began to read.

P A R T   O N E   (Scott and Susan)

Age Eight

The first time I saw the girl that would change my life forever, I wasn't very impressed. It was a Sunday, April 21, 1944. The War was raging in Europe, but to my eight-year-old eyes it was just another Sunday morning working with my dad, in Sedona, Arizona. I was in the corner of an old barn using a crowbar to pull rusty, bent nails from a pile of barn wood siding. My dad was overhead, up in the rafters, shoring up a half-broken roof beam. Raymond James, my dog, was curled up off to the side sleeping on a stack of old dry hay – his head warmed by a beam of sunlight shining through a hole in the roof.

She casually strolled in through the large open doors at the far end of the barn - kicking her feet through the straw scattered on the floor and swinging her arms forward and back. As she meandered through the barn, she calmly bent down and then jumped into the air performing a little dance maneuver that turned her halfway around before gracefully landing on one foot then the other. She looked as if she hadn't a care in the world.

She hadn't noticed my dad up in the rafters or me and Raymond James in our sheltered corner. I had stopped pulling nails and was carefully watching her every move. Raymond James had lifted his head and was equally focused on the new arrival.

She was wearing a white lace dress with polished white

shoes. Her reddish hair was tied in a ball above her head, with a few loose strands dangling down each side of her face.   As she strolled closer to where I was watching, I heard her singing quietly to herself, "Happy birthday to me, happy birthday to me, happy birth . . ." She fell silent as her eyes landed on me.

She wrinkled her brow and with an air of authority demanded, "What're you doing in my barn? My mother owns this barn and no one is supposed to be playing in here!"

I glanced up at my dad and saw that he was smiling down at us. My dad was like that, thinking it was good for me to handle situations on my own. He called them *"good learning experiences"*. But he also said that if I ever needed support, he would be there by my side.

With her hands on her hips, her legs slightly spread, looking down at me sitting on the pile of wood siding, she exclaimed, "Well?! What're you doing here? You can't play here!"

I was small for my age, a bit on the skinny side, and definitely shy and intimidated when it came to meeting pretty young girls in white lace dresses. Remembering what my dad had taught me about looking people in the eye when I was talking to them, I slowly forced my eyes up to meet hers. The first thing I noticed was how green her eyes were, not just green, but every shade and tone of green you could ever imagine, sunbursts of green that seemed to fill my small corner of the barn. Slowly I stammered, "I . . . I'm . . . not playing."

"What?! Of course you're playing. What else would you be doing?"

With a little more confidence, I pointed up to the roof rafters and said, "I'm working with my dad." My dad gave me a wink, and then to the girl, a short wave and a smile.

"You're old enough to work?" she asked with a questioning expression on her face. And then after a pause, "What are you working on?" she said with genuine interest.

*　　　*　　　*

I'd been working with my dad for as long as I can remember, spending most weekends with him on one project or another. And I use the term **work** loosely. Thinking back, I see that at first I was getting in my dad's way far more than I was actually accomplishing anything he didn't have to redo. But mostly I remember how happy I was spending time with him - the attention he gave me made me feel important.

My mother passed away while giving birth to me. I have some pictures of her and my dad has told me lots of stories - how they met, fell in love and married, but to tell you the truth, I missed the *idea* of having a mother more than missed the actual person - it's hard to miss someone you've never actually met.

It seems like every time my dad and I sat on the front porch to watch the sun melt into the horizon, he'd tell me the same story about my mother - which was okay, because it was one of my favorites. My dad would be in his old wicker rocking chair - lightly pushing with his foot, and I would be a few feet away swaying in a hammock chair hanging from the rafters. My dad would slowly take in a deep breath and then on the exhale, he'd say, "Your mother - seven months pregnant with you at the time, and I were walking through the garment district of St. Louis. It was the Christmas season and the local school was putting on the 'Christmas Carol' and needed fabric for new costumes. Your mother was asking the fabric dealers if they would be willing to contribute. While walking down the street we saw a young gentleman - a bit dirty looking, wearing old clothes, staggering across the dirt road. He then stumbled and fell face down into the gutter. The cars kept on driving by and the pedestrians looked the other way as they continued past. Everyone seemed oblivious to what had just happened. Your mother immediately ran over to where this poor fellow was lying in the road. Well maybe it wasn't quite a run, it was more like a fast waddle - her upper body was hunched forward, her legs were bowed out at the knees, and her arms were wrapped around her big belly trying to keep you from jiggling around. She was quite the sight."

My father would always stop at this point, he'd smile to himself as if seeing my mother waddle down the street for the first time . . . and then he'd continue. "We lifted this fellow onto the boardwalk and tried to help the best we could. Eventually your mother found a note in his coat pocket that said, 'I'm not drunk, I need this pill or I could die.' And sure enough there was a pill taped to that note.

"A month later at the Sunday afternoon town baseball game, your mother and I, sitting in the bleachers, saw this same fellow standing behind the backstop with a young woman and two small children. At the sight of him and his family, your mother cuddled in next to me, gave my arm a squeeze, and let out with what sounded like a little contented . . . pur-r-r-r. She had obviously given this fellow his pill."

I've heard this story so many times, I felt as if I was actually there. And in a way I guess I was . . . in my mother's belly.

At first glance, my father, being lean and strong and having a hard-edged face typically with a day or two growth of whiskers, could be a bit rough looking. But what gave away his true nature was his smile – easy and natural with lots of teeth showing. Instantly you felt like you'd been best friends forever.

My father and I came from St. Louis. He was a high school teacher and loved sharing his knowledge with his students. He had a special skill for working with the shy and lonely kids – helping them break out of their shells, helping them realize there wasn't anything they couldn't do.

When my mother died, my father was devastated. He wanted to hide from the world and for a short while he did just that, taking refuge in the one-room house he rented behind the old school where he taught. But it didn't last long. Having to raise a new born child on his own quickly brought him out of his self-imposed hibernation. In the process of learning how to raise a baby, he decided it was time to move on, start fresh, and find some place away from the noise and the hustle of the big city. He wasn't trying to run away from any bad memories – he loved his wife with all his soul and didn't want to forget a moment of their time together. His memories of being with her gave him the strength to move on.

With his worldly possessions loaded in the back of his old truck, and me, six months old, nestled in a laundry basket next to him in the front seat, we headed west with no particular destination in mind. I know you aren't supposed to have memories when you're only six months old, but I swear I remember lying in that laundry basket, the warm air from the truck's heater vent blowing on me, looking up at my dad's profile with a background of blue sky beyond, as he drove along the highway. The memory is as clear as if it were yesterday. I'm not making this up.

When we reached Sedona, my father fell in love with the place; the people were friendly and the landscape - red earth, clear streams, stunning vegetation, and fragrant air - seemed to have a pull on him. Sedona was a quiet place in the late 1930s with not much more than a few thousand people within a half day's ride. But Sedona was going through somewhat of a growth spurt. The movie industry had discovered the red rock canyons and Zane Grey, John Wayne and others came out to make their western movies. There was also the beginning of a budding colony of artists and craftsmen that moved into the area looking for inspiration from Mother Nature.

The first night we were there, my father couldn't sleep. He sat in an old wooden swinging chair on the porch of the rooming house, swaying back and forth looking up at the night sky and smelling the warm dry air carrying traces of the desert.

My father set up shop as a builder and over the years gained a reputation for doing quality work. He always said, "If a job is worth doing, it's worth doing to the best of your ability.

After all, your name will be on it." He put so much care into his projects that most clients saw him as an artist, not a builder.

*   *   *

The reddish haired girl in the white lace dress standing in the barn only a few feet in front of me, repeated, "What are you working on?"

Looking her in the eye I replied, "My dad's fixing up the barn and I'm . . ."

The girl cut me off before I could finish and chimed in, "For my mother. You're fixing up the barn for my mother."

I ignored her remarks and continued. "And I'm pulling nails out of this wood so my dad can reuse the wood for the walls." After a pause, still staring at her green eyes, I asked, "What's your name?"

Standing a little taller she said, "My name is Susan Cambell." Staring at me, she gave me a look that indicated I should be impressed. Realizing I wasn't going to say anything, she added, "What's your name?"

"Scott."

"Scott what? What's your last name?"

Standing up, I extended my hand. "Scott Montgomery. Glad to meet you." My dad had told me that I should always shake hands when I first meet someone.

With hesitation, Susan slowly reached out, grabbed my hand, squeezed tight and said, "Nice to meet you Scott Montgomery."

Sitting down on the old pile of lumber next to me, not

caring that her nice dress was getting dirty, Susan looked at me and I looked back at her.

A few feet off to the side, in the shadows, we heard a small, sharp "Woooof!"

Startled by the sudden sound of a strange animal, Susan half stood up and quickly turned in the direction of the noise. Before she had a chance to open her mouth, I quickly said, "That's Raymond James. He's my dog."

Keeping an eye on Raymond James, Susan slowly sat back down, a little closer to me this time. I could smell the fragrance of honeysuckle in her hair. Slowly a smile began to part her lips as she said, "He's kind of funny looking, what with those ears and all." A moment later, "And what kind of name is Raymond James for a dog? It sounds more like a person's name."

Having someone say Raymond James was funny looking was no big deal – it wasn't the first time I'd heard that remark. "Raymond James is not funny looking," I said. "He's unique. He's 'special' because he's the only dog that looks like that."

Raymond James, with his 'special' looking ears – one pointing straight up, the other drooping down along the side of his head, one black and one white, gave another small, "Wooof!"

"See Raymond James agrees," I said. "He's the most special dog I know. And he's named after my mother's father. His name was Raymond. My dad told me that Raymond was a funny guy that made him feel happy and good about life. And when my dad looks at Raymond James, he gets that same happy and good feeling about things, so we called him Raymond." After a pause, "And my middle name is James, so . . . Raymond James."

Glancing at Susan, I smiled and said, because I knew she was going to ask this next question, "I got Raymond James from William, he sometimes works with my dad."

One night, just around sunset, William was walking home when he found Raymond James, not more than a few months old, dirty and hungry, and skinny, barking and snarling as if he was the biggest baddest dog around. William took one look at this pint-sized dog with the big attitude and the 'special' looking ears, let out a roar of a laugh, picked up the little tyke, and the next day he gave him to me. William told me that because of his coloring and shape, a black body with white legs, chest, and snout that Raymond James was more than likely part Border Collie and part Lab.

Raymond James as if on cue, stood up, stretched, and walked over to where Susan was sitting. He sat down on his haunches, lifted his front legs onto Susan's lap, rested his head on his legs, and rolled his eyes up to meet Susan's.

Surprised, Susan looked over at me, smiled, and slowly lifted her hand to pet Raymond James' head. Raymond James' breathing slowed as he buried his head deeper into Susan's lap. After a moment, Susan still smiling said, "I think I'm going to like Raymond James . . . very much."

After a few moments of watching Susan get acquainted with Raymond James, I said, "Why are you dressed up?"

With a big smile she said, "It's my birthday, and I'm eight years old today." Reaching into a pocket of her dress, she pulled out two pieces of paper-wrapped peppermint candies. "Want one?"

Unwrapping one of the peppermints, she reached over to place it in the center of my outstretched palm. "I don't have any friends at my party. My mother and I just moved here from Chicago and I don't know anyone. There's only my mother's grown-up friends and a few of their children. That's why I came down to the barn." Susan looked down at her feet as she shuffled her polished white shoes back and forth on the dirt floor.

In an instant, before I had a chance to react, Raymond James shifted his head forward and snatched the peppermint out of my hand, then moved off a few steps to eat in private.

Susan and I broke up laughing. "He's quick," said Susan.

"Raymond James keeps you on your feet," I replied.

After a short pause, I asked, "Where's your father?" Remembering that Susan had said that she moved to Sedona with her mother . . . and not her father.

With her head down and continuing to shuffle her shoes, Susan said in a soft sad voice, "He's dead . . . of cancer."

*   *   *

Susan was born and raised in Chicago, where her father was a successful businessman importing electronics from Asia and supplying most of the retail stores up and down the east coast with inexpensive radios, tape recorders, cameras, and kitchen appliances. Her father, upon his death, left her mother financially very well off.

Susan's mother, in order to leave the sad memories of her husband's death, packed up, moved to Sedona, bought a large ranch on the outskirts of town, and began the process of forging a new life.

*   *   *

Not knowing what else to say, after hearing about her father and not having any friends at her party, I shuffled my own feet back and forth, kicking up the dirt and straw, then lowered my head and mumbled, "I'll be your friend."

Lifting her head, Susan stared at me with those deep green eyes and said in a matter-of-fact tone, "But I don't know you."

I smiled and shrugged my shoulders back at her. After a few silent seconds I said, "I also have a birthday present for you."

"You have a present for me? But you didn't even know it was my birthday!"

Standing up from the old pile of wood, I motioned for her to follow me. "Come on. It's a secret present, but you have to earn the present if you want to find it." Glancing back up at my dad, he smiled and nodded his head, indicating that it was okay for me to go.

Confused about what I was doing, Susan reluctantly followed me out through the open barn door. Raymond James, trotting along beside us, was excited to have something to do.

"What do you mean by *earn?*" Susan asked.

Outside the barn in a field of dried grass I said, "My dad says *learning* is the most important thing in life. No matter how old or young you are, you should always continue to learn as much as you can. So . . . at times he'll give me a puzzle or a game or a question to solve and at the end is a reward. My dad says a reward always means more to you if you have to earn it."

Brightening up, Susan exclaimed, "Okay, I'm good at games. What is it?"

"Okay," I repeated, pulling a piece of paper from my back pocket. "I've already solved this puzzle this morning, so I'll let you answer the questions." I read, "Start at the west corner of the barn."

I looked over at Susan. Susan looked back at me and hesitantly asked, "Which corner of the barn is west?"

Not really wanting to give her the answer, "Where does the sun set?" I smiled at her.

Looking across the dried brown field and then up at the cloudless sky, Susan pointed to a small hill covered in oaks. "The sun sets over there."

"Okay," I said. "Let's go to the corner of the barn closest to that hill."

Moving over to the near corner of the barn, I read the second clue, "How many legs does a spider have? Multiply that number by five. Facing west, in a straight line, walk that number of large steps."

Looking at Susan, I asked, "How many legs does a spider have?"

Rolling her eyes, "How would I know how many legs a spider has? I don't like spiders."

Rolling my own eyes, I replied, "Eight." Still looking at Susan, "Okay, now multiply eight by five."

"Why do we have to multiply? It's like school."

Sheepishly I said, "I got a 'C' in math and my dad says it's important to know math, so he now uses a lot of math in his puzzles."

"Forty," exclaimed Susan quickly.

Facing west, Susan and I and Raymond James marched off the forty paces across the field until we ended up standing next to a large cottonwood tree. Raymond James, running ahead of us, had beaten us to the tree and was sitting down in front of a small bush. He looked at Susan and barked, "Yelp, yelp, yelp!"

"What is Raymond James doing?" Asked Susan.

Raymond James was the smartest dog I knew, and he had been with me when I had solved the puzzle earlier. He was trying to help Susan find the answer, but I didn't want Susan to know. So I said, "Pay no attention to Raymond James, he's just playing around."

"Okay, then. So what's next?" Susan asked impatiently, anxious to find out what type of present could possibly be in this field.

I read the last clue of the puzzle, "If you are at a cottonwood, sit down facing the barn with your back against the tree. Turn your head to the left and what do you see?"

Following the directions, Susan sat against the trunk of the cottonwood and turned her head to the left - looking directly at Raymond James. "Okay, what's next?" she asked. "All I see is Raymond James."

Raymond James, hearing his name, immediately placed

his front paws on Susan's lap and then rested his head on his paws.

Susan smiled and casually without really thinking about it, as if she'd been doing it her entire life, reached over and began to scratch between Raymond James' ears.

"That's it! There are no more clues!" I said eagerly. "What else do you see?"

Squinting into the brush, Susan looked around.

With his head still on her lap, Raymond James gave Susan another quick, "Roof."

Seeing nothing of interest, she shook her head. "Nothing, I don't see anything." With mounting frustration, "Come on, what is it I'm supposed to see?"

Squatting down next to Susan, I pointed at a milkweed bush not three feet from her head, the same bush Raymond James was barking at a few moment ago. "Do you see anything?"

Looking closer, Susan countered back, "No! I don't see anything!"

"Rooof!" Raymond James barked, a little louder this time.

Raising my hand, I very slowly pointed a finger at a small green object hanging from a branch of the milkweed. Leaning in close, Susan whispered, "I can hardly see it. It looks like a piece of the branch. What is it?"

"It's a monarch butterfly. Or it will be in a week or two. Right now it's a cocoon. The monarch caterpillar turns into a cocoon, which in turn changes into a butterfly. Sometimes the monarch is called the *milkweed butterfly* because the caterpillar eats nothing but milkweed."

"That's neat," said Susan, reaching out with her finger to touch it.

"Be careful, the cocoon could break off the branch," I warned. "And then it could die."

Glancing over at me, Susan said, "How do you know so much about butterflies?"

With a hint of a smile, I said, "My dad told me."

"Your dad is pretty smart," replied Susan.

After a few silent minutes of staring at the hanging cocoon, Susan whispered, "I like it." And then, "This is a very nice birthday present. Thank you Scott Montgomery for the gift." And then, "And thank you Raymond James for helping me find it."

Raymond James knowing his name, replied, "Roooooof!"

From behind us, we heard a quick sharp voice bellow, "Susan Cambell, what are you doing out here? You're in your party dress and you're sitting in the dirt and what's all this straw all over your dress? Where have you been? This is your party and everyone is asking for the party girl!" Twenty feet behind us stood Susan's mother; tall, slim, blond, and blue eyed, her hands on her hips and a scowl on her face.

Jumping up, Susan hurried over to her mother's side and quickly said, "I don't know anyone at the party and I was bored."

Mrs. Cambell quickly brushed grass and straw from Susan's dress and fluffed up her hair. Taking a quick look over at me and Raymond James still sitting next to the milkweed bush, Mrs. Cambell turned back to Susan, bent down and whispered into her ear, "Isn't that the son of the carpenter in the barn? Why are they working on Sunday? Susan, you really shouldn't be playing with the '*help*'."

Just as Mrs. Cambell was taking hold of Susan's hand to lead her across the field back to the party, Susan turned her head towards me and said, "Okay, Scott Montgomery, I'll be your friend."

"Rooof!" said Raymond James.

One Day Later

"Look at that Mike!" said Rob, poking his elbow into the taller boy's rib cage standing next to him. "What's she wearing?"

Susan's mother had gotten Susan up early to get her ready for the first day in her new school. Susan was nervous, wondering what the other kids would be like and whether she'd make any new friends. She'd just met me the day before and hoped I would be there. After all, she did say that we could be friends.

Walking down the crowded corridor of the small three-room school house, Susan wore the uniform from her private school in Chicago - black shoes, white knee socks, a red plaid skirt and a white blouse. Looking around, Susan noticed that she was the only student in uniform. The rest of the students were dressed more casually - the boys in jeans, and flannel shirts, the girls in long skirts and wool sweaters.

Rob and Mike wove their way through the milling students until they reached Susan. Standing on each side of her, Rob and Mike, each a good nine inches taller than Susan as well as most of the other students, glared down at her.

Susan looked up at them, and hesitantly said in a low voice, not knowing what else to say, "Hi, my name is Susan."

Wrinkling his eyebrows, Mike frowned and said in a cynical voice, "What the heck are those weird clothes you have on . . . ?" And then added, " . . . Susan?"

Instantly Susan recoiled, lowered her head, and pulled her arms in tight around her chest.

"Cat got your tongue?" smirked Mike.

"Th . . . th . . . ey are my school clothes," stammered Susan, afraid of what these boys would do next.

Mike and Rob slapped each other on the back. Laughing, Mike mockingly added, "I've never seen any school clothes like that before!"

"Me neither!" hooted Rob even louder.

A small group of students formed a rough circle around the commotion as the bell rang for classes to begin. Most of the students stayed put, not wanting to miss any of the action.

From behind Susan, I walked into the circle and said, "You haven't seen clothes like that before, because you're just two small town hicks who have never been off the farm. You probably don't even know the difference between sage and mesquite." Pushing through the crowd of students, I walked up to Susan, took her by the elbow, and said, "Come on, the bells already rung."

Walking down the hall, we turned into the first classroom on the right. I said, "Don't worry about them. They always make fun of the new kids. Once you get to know them, they're not half bad."

"Oh!" Susan said, feeling a little better. "I sure hope so."

Heading to the far back corner of the room I took a seat. Following me to the back of the room, Susan remained standing, "Why're you sitting in the back? Let's sit in the front so we can hear and see the teacher better."

Realizing that I wasn't moving, Susan marched to the front of the class and took a seat directly in front of where the teacher would be standing. A few moments later, I stood up and sauntered up to the front, choosing a desk next to Susan. She turned her head towards me, looked me in the eye and slowly smiled.

"Where's Raymond James?" Susan curiously asked.

"He's sitting outside, probably under the front porch of the school." Seeing that Susan didn't quite understand, "Raymond James used to come to class with me and sit next to me under my desk, but then one day a bird flew in through the window and Raymond James started barking and chasing the bird all around the classroom, knocking over the desks. The rest of the class was hooting and hollering. It probably would have been okay, but that day was Science Day, and we had all brought in our science projects – I had made a volcano . . . that would actually erupt with lava. It was really neat. Well anyway, with the bird flying around, and Raymond James chasing it, and the desks being knocked over, all the science projects got . . . pretty much destroyed. And even that may not have been that bad, except the teacher didn't know what grades to give us because all our science projects were ruined. We all had to rebuild our projects, which put the class behind schedule which the teacher didn't like." Looking at Susan, I rolled my eyes, "So all the teachers had a meeting and they decided it would be best if Raymond James stayed outside during class."

Susan sat staring at me with her mouth hanging open. She seemed stunned, feeling sorry for Raymond James.

"It's okay." I said to break the silence. "Raymond James mostly sleeps when I'm in class and he can sleep under the porch as well as under my desk. And I see him at lunch and during recess . . . so it's okay."

Recovering quickly, Susan said, "Oh . . . well okay. As long as Raymond James is okay." And then a moments later, leaning closer to me, "What is the difference between sage and mesquite?"

Looking back at her, I said, "Everything is different. Sage is a bush that smells like the herb and mesquite is a tree that smells like a musty pine. They aren't even close. I just said it because I knew Mike and Rob wouldn't know what they were."

Smiling at me, Susan cocked her head to one side and gave me a questioning look.

Staring back, I said, "Yeah, my dad told me."

"Oh-h-h-h. Just what I thought," grinned Susan

*   *   *

For the rest of the school day, I stayed by Susan's side, not to protect her from the bullies, or from any obligation I felt to introduce her to my friends – which I did, or because I wanted to play with her during recess – which I also did, or to eat lunch with her – again which I did, but because I . . . just . . . I guess I just felt comfortable being with her. It felt like I was where I belonged.

At the sound of the final bell, Susan and I rushed out of the school building and Raymond James rushed out from under the porch. Raymond James was happy to see us and we were happy to see him, as he jumped, and barked, and ran in circles around us. I was glad and somewhat amazed at how fast Raymond James had taken to Susan. It was if the three of us had been together our entire lives, not just a day.

At the school gate, Susan abruptly turned left and preceded a good ten feet along the path, Raymond James by her side, before I had a chance to ask, "Where're you going?"

Turning back to face me she said, "Home . . . aren't you coming?" Without saying anything, she had naturally assumed that I would walk home with her, which . . . made me feel good.

Confused about the direction she was walking, I said, "Well, yeah I'm coming, but your house is this way," Pointing in the opposite direction.

"Oh?" Susan said, as she and Raymond James turned and sauntered back to where I was standing - a big smile on her face, as if making a wrong turn was no big deal.

Together we headed off down the road to her house. Along the way we talked and laughed, and I even managed to find a sage bush and a mesquite tree so that Susan could see the difference between the two. When we reached her driveway, we stopped to say our goodbyes. Susan knelt down and placed her forehead on Raymond James forehead and with both hands scratched under his ears. "You're absolutely the best dog in the world," She said. "The absolute best." And then to my surprise, Susan quickly stood up, leaned over towards me, and gave me a kiss; not a peck on the cheek, but square on the lips. It wasn't a very long kiss, but it sure was nice. With a suggestion of a smile on her face, Susan shyly said, "Thanks for making my first day of school fun." She turned and quickly walked up the drive.

I was stunned. I had just been kissed for the first time, and I wasn't sure what to do. I stood there in a fog, watching Susan fade around the near bend in the drive. Just before she disappeared, I shouted, "Don't forget to wear a long skirt and sweater tomorrow instead of your school uniform!"

Nine Years Later: Juniors in High School, Age Seventeen

Talking to no one in particular, Manuel said, "I think the gun sights were off."

"What're you talking about?" groaned Maria in a loud voice. "Even I knocked down more ducks than you did in the shooting gallery and look at what Scott won for Susan!"

Susan raised her eyebrows and smiled as she held up a large fluffy gray hippopotamus with small black eyes.

After a sip of soda Maria added, "Where's my Hippo?"

Sitting at a picnic table, munching on burgers and sodas, we all laughed as Manuel sheepishly shrugged his shoulders and shook his head.

Once a year a traveling carnival made its way through our small town of Sedona, complete with your classic strong man, bearded lady, house of mirrors, a two-headed bull, a Ferris wheel, giant swings, shooting galleries, dart throwing, and all the rest. Every year, Susan and I and our friends, Manuel and Maria, managed to spend our money and have fun. Typically we wouldn't leave until the roustabouts threw us out at closing.

Load noises and bright lights usually made Raymond James a little jumpy, so I typically left him at home. But today Susan had caved in. Raymond James' whimpering and pleading eyes were no match for Susan's will power. I swear that dog had Susan wrapped around his paw. Bottom line, Raymond James was lying under our table, pressed tightly to my foot - he liked to be in contact with me whenever he was in unfamiliar surroundings. Raymond James was quiet, but on full alert - aware of all that was going on around him.

*   *   *

Ever since Susan and I first met in the barn on her eighth birthday some nine years ago, hardly a day has gone by that we haven't been together or at least talked or made contact in some way. Yes, I know that we lived in the same small town, went to the same small school, had the same small circle of friends, but it was more than that. It was like some invisible magnetic force pulled us together. Whenever we were separated, this force would reach out, across the town or across the countryside, and make a connection. I could feel her presence even when we weren't together.

We were alike in so many ways; we both saw the humor in life and loved to laugh. We enjoyed reading almost anything as long as it wasn't boring. We enjoyed watching movies from the back row of the movie house, munching on popcorn. We enjoyed helping people – Susan more on a larger scale, me more one-on-one. We both liked to touch, not necessarily sexually but just to be in physical contact with each other; holding hands, arms around the waist, shoulders touching as we watched a movie, leaning into each other as we read, or intertwining our legs as we lay on a blanket under a tree doing homework.

But it wasn't just our similarities that brought us close. We had a lot of differences and these differences seemed to balance out the things we had in common. I was more logical in my decision-making. Susan abandoned logic and was more into her feelings, often saying, "It *feels* right." The funny thing was Susan's feelings were right more often than not. I was more on the quiet side; happy to listen, to observe, to ask questions, and to learn about the other guy. Susan was more into talking, telling me about her day and how she felt about things. I liked to explore, discovering what was around the next bend, trying to figure out what made things tick, and as Susan stated on many occasions, "Scott, you ask a heck of a lot of questions." Susan liked routine and being around familiar settings. If she was comfortable, she would stay the course and not want to sway to the right or to the left . . . at least not much.

*   *   *

"What's next?" exclaimed Susan, sitting at the picnic table at the carnival. And then with a sexy smile added, "I'm up for the Tunnel of Love."

"What about the giant swing?" piped in Manuel.

Maria, giving Manuel a stern look, "Oh come on! We've already been on the swings and now after we've eaten all this junk, no telling what will happen." Maria, pressing on her stomach, leaned forward, opened her mouth and pretended to throw up.

Smiling, Susan turned to me and without saying a word gave me, 'the look'. The look that said, "W-e-e-e-l-l Scott, what's your choice?"

Knowing full well I didn't really have a choice, I smiled back at Susan, chuckled and said, "Looks like it's the Tunnel of Love."

Gathering up the food wrappers and paper cups, we threw them in the trash barrel and strolled over towards the Tunnel of Love. Raymond James by my side, occasionally pressing against my leg, closely observing everything going on around him.

We maneuvered our way through the crowd; wide-eyed, scampering, screaming kids charged up on cotton candy, sodas, and popcorn running all around; parents trying to keep track of their kids; couples with men trying to impress their ladies at the next game of skill; and the older folks meandering along the sidelines, smiling and trying to take it all in. The colored lights surrounding the main boardwalk blinked brightly, the music from the rides blared loudly, screams from the thrill riders echoed off the tents, and the smell of popcorn, straw, and sweets filled our senses.

Off to the left, a fast talking voice over at the Shooting Gallery shouted, "Come on boys, ten cents will get you ten shots, knock down only five ducks and you can have your choice of any of these f-i-i-i-i-ne stuffed animals."

Manuel, slowing his pace, turned to see the man waving his arm at the rows of stuffed animals. "Maybe we can have another try at the Shooting Gal . . ."

Before Manuel had a chance to finish his thought, Maria put her arms around Manuel's waist and with a little effort guided him in the opposite direction away from the shooting gallery. "You've already spent enough money trying to win me a stuffed hippo. It's time for the Tunnel of Love!" she shouted over the noise.

With my arm around Susan's shoulder and Raymond James at my feet, the four of us waited in line to board the small boats that would take us on our journey through the Tunnel of Love. Over the sounds of the music and the screams of the thrill riders, I said in a loud voice to our small group, "Are we still on for the hike this Saturday? My dad told me about a great place. It should be fun."

I'd always felt a connection with the land surrounding Sedona. Being in nature, smelling the pines and sage and wet earth, feeling the heat or coolness of the seasons, observing the smallest insect or the largest buck as they went about their lives. I enjoyed exploring the canyons and plateaus, following a stream up a ravine until I found its origin, or coming across a hidden Indian site high up the side of a sandstone cliff and then realizing that I was more than likely the first person in over a few hundred years to step foot on that spot. Being out in nature recharged my batteries and I wanted to share my experience with others so I was always trying to get Susan and my friends to come along with me on the hikes.

"Thanks, buddy, I know I said I would go, but it's the busy season at the restaurant and it'll be packed. I've got to help my parents," responded Manuel, patting me on the back. "Otherwise, I'd be there."

"Sorry Scott," Maria said with a frown. "I've got to take care of my sister's baby. Out of the blue, she and her husband decided to take a trip to Las Vegas. They're calling it an early wedding anniversary."

Looking at Susan, I gave her my best puppy dog expression.

"I can't," Susan exclaimed. "You know I tutor kids on the Reservation on Saturdays."

Susan enjoyed giving to others; helping out at the orphanage in Flagstaff, volunteering at food drives, donating clothes, and tutoring kids on the Reservation who were having a tough time keeping up in school. I had forgotten.

"What about Sunday?" I quickly added looking at Susan. "I need to help my dad on Sunday over at the old town hall, but I can switch to Saturday and hike on Sunday."

A bit embarrassed Susan slowly said, "My mother has" swallowing before she continued, "arranged for me to meet the son of one of her friends from Phoenix this Sunday."

"Oh man, are you kidding?" said Manuel. "Your mom is still trying to break you and Scott up? That's wacky!"

Maria, sounding frustrated, "Why doesn't she like Scott? He's the best."

Manuel nudged Maria and gave her a questioning look. Maria nudged Manuel back and with a sly smile said, "I mean, Scott's the best . . . other than you Manuel."

I remained quiet. I'd heard it all before.

Susan added, "It's not that my mother doesn't like Scott. It's just that she wants the best for me."

"Better than my best pal, Scott?!" shouted Manuel.

Susan grimaced, "My mother wants me to be secure and safe from . . . I don't know . . . I guess life's mishaps and she thinks money will give me those things. I hate to say it but she wants me to be with someone who has lots of money."

"Absolutely wacky!" howled Manuel. "Wacky!"

Susan slid her arm through mine and leaned in close, "I go on these dates to humor my mom and to keep the peace, but Scott knows I belong to him."

After a few moments of awkward silence, I said, "Hey, enough already. We're here to have fun. Let's climb aboard the Tunnel of. . . " and then in a deep slow voice, "L-o-o-o-v -e." I took Susan's hand, we had made it to the front of the line, and stepped over and onto the small boat that would take us on our journey through *romance*.

Looking back at Raymond James, I gave him a serious look and in a stern voice said, "STAY." Raymond James immediately walked to the side of the entrance and lay down - half covered by the flap of the tent.

An elderly man dressed in well worn, loose fitting clothes and a floppy hat that had taken our tickets, nodded at me and said, "Not to worry. I'll keep an eye on him."

I smiled and nodded back, knowing that Raymond James didn't need anyone to 'keep an eye on him'. "Thanks." I said.

Susan and I settled back into the small boat, Manuel and Maria one boat behind. As we gently glided along the man-made stream, soft music quietly filled the air, and dimly lit images of fully dressed couples in various romantic poses appeared to our left and right. Susan and I chuckled at the poor attempt of creating a romantic atmosphere. The most romantic part of the ride for me was sitting next to the person I cared most about, Susan.

In school, Rob and Mike had told me about 'the move' they had used many times before on their dates and said it was a sure winner. I had my doubts but figured now was as good a time as any to give it a try. Turning my head away from Susan so she couldn't see, I opened my mouth wide and practiced my *fake yawn.* "Not bad," I said to myself. "Okay, here goes." Slowly I stretched my arms out wide, arched my head back, fake yawned, and then slowly let my right arm drift down towards Susan's shoulders.

Out of the corner of her eyes, Susan watched as I made 'the move'. With my arm almost around her shoulders, she reached out and punched me in the stomach. "Sometimes you are the weirdest person I know. Was that the '*fake stretch move*', Rob and Mike were telling everyone about in school? How could you listen to those two bananas?" Grabbing my arm and cuddling in close she said. "How many times have you put your arm around me? Hundreds and hundreds of times. You don't need any 'move' to get close to me."

She looked at me and I looked at her. After a few seconds we broke up laughing. After a few more seconds we both instantly stopped laughing and listened.

"Did you hear that?" I asked. "It sounded like someone fell in the water."

"Yeah. Something definitely fell in the water," replied Susan."

We both listened carefully to see if we could hear anything else. There was definitely a rhythmic, splash-splash . . . splash-splash . . . splash-splash off in the distance, but we couldn't make out what it was. The splashing was getting closer and before we knew it the "splash-splash" was right beside us. In the next instant, from out of the darkness sprang two white paws from the water that landed directly in front of us on the side of our little boat, followed quickly by the head of Raymond James, and two short, "Wooof! Wooof's!"

I don't know who was happier: Raymond James barking excitedly, licking our faces, and shaking water all over us, or Susan and I laughing so hard our sides ached.

It was the best ride of the day.

*   *   *

Susan's Mother was born in Chicago on what she calls the wrong side of the tracks. Susan's grandmother cleaned houses for the wealthy and Susan's grandfather was a handyman that pushed a cart full of tools along the road, swinging a bell and advertising his skills by hollering to the houses as he passed. Susan's grandparents knew how the wealthy lived and wanted the same for their daughter (Susan's mother). When Susan's mother came of age, even though her parents couldn't afford it, she was given all the latest in clothing fashions, the newest hair styles, and studied the latest topics in conversation. She attended all the best parties, sometimes invited, sometimes not. She went to all the Saturday Socials and made sure to dance with and schmooze with the wealthiest of the eligible boys. Because of Susan's mother's training and her tall slim figure and blond hair, it didn't take long before she had snagged a prime candidate. They were quickly married.

Susan's mother, now a widow but having money and plenty of contacts, wanted the same for her daughter.

*   *   *

Two days later, I had planned to go on the hike by myself and of course with Raymond James, since everyone at the carnival a couple nights before had said they had other plans. As we approached the trailhead, Raymond James ran ahead. A smile came to me as I heard the barking of Raymond James echo off the nearby sandstone cliffs. There was a very specific tone in Raymond James' bark whenever he was with Susan . . . and I was now hearing that bark.

I was very, very happy when I saw Susan waiting at the trailhead sitting on a tree stump - her legs crossed at the knees and her right foot impatiently bobbing up and down. A knapsack leaning against the stump, I assumed, was stuffed full of food, drinks and blankets. Raymond James sat by her side on all fours impatiently looking at me as he gave me a bark that said, "Hurry up. What's taking you so long? Susan's here and we have a hike to get to."

Walking over to Susan, I said with a questioning look on my face, "How'd you get out of the blind date with . . . MacDuck or MacFuddle or Mac . . . whatever his name is?" I was in good spirits now that Susan was coming along.

"Don't be mean," answered Susan. "You know his name is MacTwidle. It's an old family name that goes way back, and he's very nice."

After staring at each other for a few silent moments, Susan cracked a smile, jumped off the log, ran towards me, and jumped up into my arms. We broke-up laughing. "MacTwidle?" I said, laughing even louder.

Raymond James ran around barking with excitement,

Giggling to herself, Susan explained, "I got out of the blind date by helping my mother see the light. I explained to her that it was futile for her to try and set me up with someone else because you, Scott Montgomery, are the only one for me. And believe it or not, I think she's finally accepted it."

"Yeah, that'll be the day. And by helping your mother 'see the light', do you mean you cried and whined and threw a fit until she didn't have any choice but to give in?"

"You got it," chuckled Susan as she turned and started up the trail dressed in a pair of well-worn leather boots laced half way up her calves, a baggy pair of tattered shorts, and a loose fitting buttoned down shirt. Her reddish hair was tucked beneath a wide-brimmed straw hat.

I watched Susan from behind as she sashayed up the trail, swinging her hips from side to side and waving her arms front to back as if she hadn't a care in the world, Raymond James happily by her side.

"Don't forget the knapsack," she shouted back to me

*   *   *

When Raymond James and I hiked by ourselves, we typically moved along at a pretty fast pace and I brought just enough water and food for us to make it through the hike. When Susan came along, we moved at a much slower pace, sightseeing along the way, and we typically brought a knapsack full of picnic supplies. Susan would usually walk in front, Raymond James by her side, and me a few paces behind. When the trail hit an uphill incline, I would give Susan a little extra help by placing my hand on her backside and pushing. As I pushed, forward and upward, she would lean back into my push, saying, "This is great, like sitting in a chair floating up the trail." After a while I was not only pushing on the uphills, but also on the flats. I didn't mind.

Raymond James would always walk alongside Susan, as if he instinctively knew that Susan's focus was on enjoying the scenery – the landscape, the sky, the rock formations, the wildlife, and not on watching where she was stepping. Raymond James was there to kind of . . . protect Susan from stepping in a hole, or tripping over a stray branch, or walking too close to the edge of a cliff. On one occasion when we were hiking a little known trail in the back side of a box canyon, Raymond James suddenly grabbed hold of Susan's shoe and pulled her back down the trail towards me. He then stepped in front of Susan, as if trying to block her from moving any further. Raymond James then moved twenty feet down the trail, crouched down into an attack position, focused all his senses on something straight ahead, and emitted a growl that came from somewhere deep within. I cautiously came up behind him and almost instantly the sound of a vibrating rattle came from a snake not more than ten feet in front of us smack dab in the middle of the trail.

With Susan looking up at the top of the cliffs and the cloud formations, there was no telling what would have happened if Raymond James hadn't stopped us before reaching the snake.

And yes I took a long stick, gently pushed the angry snake – we had disturbed its warming afternoon nap - off the trail and watched it slide off into the bushes.

*   *   *

Fifteen minutes into our hike, coming to a fork in the trail, Susan asked, "Okay, which way do we go?"

"Hold on, let me check the directions." Reaching back to pull a piece of crumpled brown paper from my back pocket, I read, "Step One: *Che-Ah-Chi.*" Grinning from ear to ear, I looked over at Susan.

Susan asked, "Another one of your father's puzzles?"

"Yep."

*   *   *

My dad always believed the most important thing in life was to learn. As he got a bit older, he expanded his philosophy to include: we not only need to learn, but we also need to share what we've learned with others and have fun in the process. By sharing with others, we add to what they know and then they can pass it on to others, who can then add to it and pass it on again and again and again. If his thinking is correct, eventually someone should know everything.

My dad got the directions for our hike from William, his close friend and a very skilled woodworker. William was an Apache Indian who had lived in and around the Sedona area for many years. He was at least six feet six inches tall and weighed close to three hundred pounds. He looked big, mean, and tough, but his friends knew him as a very kind, gentle and giving soul. Also, if you remember . . . William is the one who found Raymond James in the desert and was nice enough to give him to me.

William had asked my dad to pass the directions for the hike on to me. William knew that I loved to explore the canyons and hills around Sedona. He told my dad that the hike would be a very special experience. As expected, my dad put William's directions into the form of a puzzle.

*   *   *

"What happens if we can't figure out the directions from the puzzle?" questioned Susan.

"Then it will be a nice short hike rather than a nice long

hike." After a pause, "But I'm confident we'll figure it out."

With a mischievous look, Susan said, "You don't think I know what the first clue means, do you?"

Lifting my eyebrows, I gave Susan a half smirk and said, "You should. We've talked about *Che-Ah-Chi* enough times."

"I know exactly what *Che-Ah-Chi* is, and where *Che-Ah-Chi* is. Just follow me!" called out Susan as she and Raymond James turned up the trail, confidently taking the right fork and ambling a good twenty paces along the trail before turning around to see that . . . I hadn't moved.

"It's this way," I said shaking my head and pointing in the opposite direction; the left fork.

＊   ＊   ＊

Susan had the uncanny ability to always, and I mean always, turn the opposite way we wanted to go. When we would leave the school house, the movies, the bowling alley, a friend's house, you name it, she would inevitably turn the wrong way when we left. One time when we exited the library, Susan turned right to go to my truck, which was parked only a short distance to the left. I decided not to say anything, and walked beside her to see just how far she'd go before realizing that the truck was in the opposite direction. We continued, casually talking, until we reached the corner where she confidently turned left, and then another left at the next corner before she stopped, looked around, looked at me, and said somewhat surprised, "Where's the truck?"

I cracked up with laughter and said, "Where did you

think you were going?"

Shaking her head, she said, "I didn't think anything. I just started walking."

Still laughing, I said, "Well the truck was in the opposite direction you walked."

"Really? Well, where is it now?"

Because Susan had walked us in a circle around the block, we had ended up back in front of the library and only a short distance from the truck. Pointing a few feet ahead, I said, "It's right there."

Beaming with delight, Susan exclaimed, "See, I knew exactly where I was going."

I put my arm around her shoulders, chuckled to myself, and slowly shook my head. "Susan you're the greatest."

*   *   *

Thirty minutes into our hike, about a mile up the trail, Susan wondering if we were heading in the right direction, asked, "What's the next clue?"

Remembering what **Step Three** was from the last time I looked at my dad's directions, I said without pulling the folded brown paper from my pocket, "Follow the medicine wheel."

"You sure?"

"I'm sure."

"So we get to the medicine wheel, and the medicine wheel will tell us where to go?"

"That's it."

"But where's the medicine wheel?" Susan asked, as she

took a few steps towards me and pulled a canteen of water from the knapsack slung over my left shoulder.

Noticing that we had stopped, Raymond James strolled over to the shade of a nearby scrub oak and lay down for a quick rest.

"I don't know," I responded, taking hold of the canteen as Susan took a swallow and passed it to me.

"What'd you mean, you don't know? How are we supposed to find a medicine wheel out here in the middle of nowhere?"

I smiled and said, "It's easy, just **think**, medicine wheel. Hold the **thought** of a medicine wheel in your head and then our thoughts will focus in and lead us straight to it."

Susan, scrunching up her nose, as if questioning my intelligence, said, "In other words, we'll be crawling through the brush, blindly looking at everything we can as we search from here to Timbuktu."

"We'll find it," I said poking Susan in the side.

"Ummmph," mumbled Susan. And then under her breath added, "I bet this is going to be a short hike."

*   *   *

"Come on, Susan. You can make it. Put your right foot on that round rock and give me your left hand. I'll pull and you push with your foot."

Breathing hard, Susan extended her left arm and on the count of three we pulled and pushed and struggled and eventually she lunged upward the last few feet and landed squarely on top of me.

Winded, Susan coughed, "Thanks for the soft landing."

We had found the medicine wheel fifteen minutes before, carved into the face of a large boulder set into the side of a small sandstone cliff. Our trail had dead-ended at the face of the red sandstone cliff and it wasn't until we began pushing the overgrown brush aside that we discovered the medicine wheel. I was somewhat surprised it took so long to find the medicine wheel – typically my dad's clues were a lot easier to follow. The medicine wheel had a spoke that passed beyond the boundary of the wheel. We figured the spoke was pointing in the direction we should follow. The problem was, the spoke pointed straight up. Searching the area, we found no signs of any trails leading around the sides of the cliffs, so we huffed and we puffed and we climbed – straight up. Or I should say, I huffed and I puffed and I climbed and I sweated, and then I pulled Susan up after me until we reached the top of the cliff.

And now that we had made it to the top, with Susan sitting comfortably on my stomach, I gasped, "Good job Susan. I couldn't have done it without you."

Patting the side of my leg, Susan out of breath, said, "Oh, it was nothing."

Raymond James had somehow found his own way up the face of the small cliff and seeing that Susan was sitting on top of me, decided it would be a good idea to join the party. Raymond James ran over to Susan, jumped on her lap, slightly knocking her backwards in the process, gave her face a couple quick licks, and then lifted his head and started howling to the wind. The whole time his tail was swinging back and forth, slapping me across the face.

"All right, all right already. Come on Raymond James, give me a break with this tail." I grabbed hold of Raymond James' tail and added, "I'm glad we're having fun guys, but I think it's time to move on." I slid out from under Susan and Raymond James and dusted myself off.

"Let us know when you've found the trail," smiled Susan. "Raymond James and I will take a quick break".

Raymond James let us know that he agreed with Susan by giving us a quick, "Yelp, Yelp." He rested his front legs and head on Susan's lap, as she poured some water into a cup for him to enjoy.

I explored the area, but all I saw was a thick grove of overgrown, dried brush. Eventually I found something that vaguely resembled a trail – a small opening between lots of scratchy brush that led off into a sea of thicker scratchy brush.

"Are we going through that?" said Susan as she made a face that told me, no way was she going in there.

"I'll lead the way and try to clear a path. Stay close behind so that the branches don't swing back and hit you."

As I started through the brush, Susan jumped onto my back and squealed, "Is this close enough?"

Laughing, I replied, as I plowed through the brush, "That's perfect."

Susan tucked her head between my shoulder blades, closed her eyes, and held on tight. Raymond James followed closely behind. The ground was fairly level and for some reason, even after the long hike, Susan felt as light as a feather. This place had energized me.

Thirty yards in, the brush abruptly ended at the face of another red sandstone cliff, much taller than the one we had just climbed. Still riding on my back, Susan said, "Where to now?"

Not sure which way to go, I scanned the face of the red wall to the left and then back to the right. Maybe ten feet along the base of the cliff to the right I saw what appeared to be a narrow slot cut smoothly into the cliff. The opening looked as if it had been formed by flowing water from above and was hidden behind a pile of fallen red boulders. Dropping Susan to the ground, we slowly made our way along the base of the cliff - the rough sandstone rubbing us raw on one side and the dry brush scratching us red on the other. Reaching the gap, we turned sideways and carefully moved, small step after small step, through the opening. Twenty feet in, the slot ended and we stepped into what . . . I can only describe as . . . *another world.*

Eyes wide and mouth open, Susan slowly said, "Wow!" A few moments later, I repeated, "Wo-o-o-o-w." Raymond James, standing between us, was unusually calm and quiet. The slot gap had opened into a gorgeous sandstone grotto. The grotto was circular in shape, maybe two hundred feet across, with one section of the circle missing, opening out into a spectacular view of Sedona, the desert, and beyond. The sandstone walls, at least one hundred and fifty feet tall, had been sculptured by the wind and the rain into smooth feminine curves. The horizontal layers of sandstone alternated from red, to orange, to yellow, to brown and then back to red, orange, yellow, brown. On the back side of the grotto, opposite the opening to the view, amongst an outcropping of red sandstone boulders, was a small pond with water trickling down a series of flat stones into a larger irregular shaped pool, maybe twenty feet across. The water sparkled like diamonds from the reflections of the high afternoon sun. The floor of the grotto was mostly fine pink sand with an occasional island of green grass and pockets of shrubbery lining the base of the sandstone cliffs. But what made this grotto so unique, so wonderful, so delightful was the majestic giant cottonwood that stood almost dead center. The tree was well over two hundred feet tall with branches spreading a good one hundred feet in all directions. A slight breeze swayed the leaves of the cottonwood, gently coaxing thousands of white delicate seed pods to float silently to the ground. The rose colored sand around the base of the cottonwood was covered in a thin blanket of white cotton-like seeds. This magnificent cottonwood was the guardian of the grotto, spreading its branches to protect all who ventured within.

The distant views; the smooth sandstone cliffs; the sounds of trickling water; the soft carpet of snowy cottonwood petals; the mixed smells of damp sand, dry brush, cottonwood and sage were intoxicating. It was a world of its own - a paradise.

Susan and I stood just inside the slot awed by the sights, and sounds, and smells.

"It's magical," whispered Susan, trying not to disturb the peacefulness of the grotto.

"I've never seen anything like it," I whispered back. "It feels as if we're in church - the most beautiful church in the world."

Taking my hand, Susan led us forward to explore the grotto in more detail. We discovered that the ponds were fed by a hidden spring. We saw plenty of reeds and moss and small frogs and insects skimming across the surface, but no fish.

We stood under the cottonwood with our arms spread wide and our heads tilted back looking up at the sky as the soft white seeds drifted down onto our faces. We noticed a few small birds darting in and out of the branches and a few monarch butterflies fluttering from the pond to the tree and then back to the pond. We saw no evidence of any kind that another human had ever stepped foot into this wonderland.

Eventually, we picked a grassy spot below the outer edges of the overhanging cottonwood branches that overlooked the valley below, spread our blanket and unpacked our lunch.

Raymond James meanwhile had found a spot directly in front of the Cottonwood, not more than five feet from the base of the tree, lay down, rested his head on his front paws and instantly fell asleep. It was the most peaceful looking sleep I had ever seen any creature have (human or animal). It was as if Raymond James was sleeping with Mother Nature by his side.

Sitting cross-legged on the blanket, overlooking a distant Sedona, Susan pulled a couple of bologna sandwiches wrapped in wax paper from the knapsack and said, "How is it that no one else besides William and maybe your father, if William ever took him here, knows about this place? It's so beautiful."

Taking hold of the sandwich that Susan offered, I unfolded the waxed paper and took a bite. After I swallowed, I said, "Well, we had directions and we still had a tough time finding it. Plus climbing the cliff and struggling through the brush wasn't a cakewalk. It's unlikely that anyone would just stumble upon this place." After another bite, "And you can't see the grotto from below and the sandstone cliffs hide it from the surrounding hills. The only way to see it is if you fly directly overhead and even then you'd have to come back and find it on foot." After a pause, "It's good that no one knows about this place. If they did, it would be overrun with people. I like it just the way it is."

Susan cuddled up next to me, wrapped her hands around my arm and rested her head on my shoulder. Neither of us said a word, we sat together quietly looking off into the distance.

A few minutes later, with Susan still resting her head on my shoulder, she softly said, "This is our 'special place'. Let's not tell anyone about it. This place will be just for us."

I moved around on the blanket until I sat face to face with her. I leaned forward and wrapped my arms around her and whispered into her ear, "I agree. This will be our 'special place'."

A moment later, she whispered, "I love you."

I quickly responded in a tender voice, "I love you," and then added, "More . . . I love you more."

Smiling, Susan said, "How much more?"

Thinking about it, I replied, "More than all the stars in the universe."

In a soft whisper, I heard Susan mumble, "I love you twice that much."

With our arms wrapped around each other and our heads side by side, I closed my eyes and took in a deep breath, the scent of Susan and a hint of sage filled my nostrils. On the exhale, every muscle in my body relaxed and I felt the tension and fatigue slide down my limbs and dissolve into the earth. My thoughts quieted, my worries disappeared, and a wave of . . . something I can only describe as . . . *complete harmony* with the grotto rolled over me. I felt so very, very at ease with myself and my surroundings - not just a physical ease but an emotional and mental ease that touched the very center of my being.

Feeling Susan's body pressed against my body, I knew beyond a shadow of a doubt that Susan and I were supposed to be together, not just for today but . . . forever. At that moment there was no difference between who I was and who Susan was - my arm was her arm, my leg was her leg, my heart was her heart, and my thoughts were her thoughts. I felt at peace and was enveloped in a feeling of knowing that everything was exactly the way it was supposed to be. Slowly, Susan and I faded away.

I'm not sure how long we stayed in this embrace - whether a few seconds or a few lifetimes - but eventually I heard the distant chatter of a scrub jay and, as I gradually returned my awareness to the red sandstone grotto, I realized the jay was no more than a foot away, skipping from branch to branch in a small sage bush. Eventually settling on a branch directly in front of my face, the jay stood perfectly still, staring into my eyes as I stared back into its small black eyes. For a split second, the jay seemed familiar. I'm not sure how to explain it . . . as if we were close friends. And then the moment passed and the jay bobbed its head once and then several times from side to side, before opening its beak and giving one loud squawk, as if scolding me, before it hopped off the branch, spread its wings and gently soared away. Watching the scrub jay disappear down the distant valley, I turned back to the grotto where everything seemed brighter, newer, as if I was seeing life for the first time. A soft white halo encircled the giant cottonwood with Raymond James asleep at its base.

Susan still sat in front of me and our arms were still wrapped around each other as I turned my head towards her - she was glowing, a rainbow of colors surrounded her head. Her eyes, open wide, were a sunburst of bright greens. We gazed at each other for maybe a few seconds or maybe for an eternity – I didn't know, time had disappeared.

Susan, squeezing her arms a little tighter around my shoulders, leaned forward and gently placed her lips on mine. Her tongue found my tongue, her nails softly dug into my back, and I tasted the sweet warmth of her lips. Without a thought about what I was doing, our lips still moving as one, I began to unbutton her shirt. After the top few buttons, I reached in and cradled the underside of her supple, smooth breast. I heard a low moan as we rolled back onto the blanket.

*   *   *

Sometime later, Susan and I, lying naked on the blanket, looked up at the bright blue cloudless sky.   At our sides our hands touched and our fingers interlocked. The rays of the sun warmed our bare bodies and a light breeze rustled the leaves of the cottonwood, blanketing us with falling white seed petals - like warm snow slowing drifting down from the sky. The smell of sage filled the air and a few monarch butterflies floated by.

Eventually I rolled over onto my elbow and with a big smile gazed into Susan's eyes and slowly said, "Wow!"

Susan smiled back and repeated, "Wow!"

She pulled my head down and gently brushed my cheek with her lips as she softy whispered into my ear, "Our 'special place'."

End Of Part One

Sitting on the floor, underneath the sunlit window in the library of the old building, Mathew slowly placed the last of the old frail sheets of paper face down on his lap. The sun was quickly setting and the room was slowly changing from filtered sunlight to soft gray.

With a slow exhale, Mathew said, "Well . . . that's it."

Sitting on the floor next to Mathew, leaning together, shoulder to shoulder, Amanda abruptly pushed herself away from him and said in a frustrated tone, "What do you mean, that's it? Where's the rest of the story? What happened to Scott and Susan?"

Shrugging, Mathew replied, "That's all there is. There's no more."

"No way can this Scott Montgomery leave us hanging." Picking up the oilcloth resting next to Mathew, Amanda folded the cover back and looked inside. "What's this?" she exclaimed, pulling out a single remaining sheet. "I thought there wasn't any more paper?" Amanda read:

Hello, whoever you are.

I have no idea if anyone will ever find my story or if it is found whether anyone will be interested in reading it. I figured there was a pretty good chance it would end up in the town dump or someone's fireplace. I hid our story in my old desk because I didn't want just anyone to find it. What Susan and I had was very special and I only wanted to share our story with someone equally as special who would appreciate our relationship. And if you are now reading this and are still interested then you must in some way value the bond that Susan and I had. You must have been drawn to our story – how else could you have discovered my hiding place? You must admit it was a pretty darn good hiding place.

So whoever you are, if you've read this far, then you know that my dad liked to use puzzles, stories, scavenger hunts, and other games as a means to help teach. He would say, "If you earn the knowledge then you'll value it that much more." Well, in honor of my dad, you're going to have to earn the right to read about the most precious person in my life, Susan. You'll find that she's well worth the effort.

What I've done is divide the story into several parts; you've just finished Part One. At the end of each Part, I will give you a clue that will lead you to the next installment of our story. It's that simple. If you're still intrigued and wish to continue, take a look at the following clue.

The best of everything and don't forget to learn, share and enjoy.

Scott Montgomery

Amanda looked up at Mathew, and in a questioning voice asked, "What do you think? Are we going on a scavenger hunt?"

"Of course we are," Mathew responded, surprised that Amanda was even thinking about stopping. "How else are we going to find out what happened to Scott and Susan?"

Smiling, Amanda added, "Just checking."

Clue No. One

When I was a kid, my dad told me a story. He said it was about friendship. I have forgotten the exact words, but it went something like this:

A long, long time ago before the Great Shaman created his People of Sedona, before the land had fully dried from the disappearance of the great lake, in a time where all the animals spoke the same language, there was a snake and a rat. The snake and the rat shared the same patch of ground, breathed the same air, rested below the same trees, and became friends. All of the other rats couldn't believe that this rat had a snake as a friend. They told this rat that the snake would eat it. But the rat refused to believe them because the snake was his friend. All the other snakes couldn't understand why this snake hadn't eaten this rat, but the snake refused to eat the rat because the rat was his friend.

A winter came along that was very bad. The rat survived on insects and acorns, but there was no food for the snake. There came a time when the snake couldn't take it any longer and had to eat. The snake decided to eat his friend, the rat. Recognizing the snake's intent, the rat scurried down a hole. The snake slithered down after the rat. The rat ran out an escape hole, across the field and down another hole. When the snake stuck his head out of the escape hole to look around in search of the rat, he saw standing next to him the Great Shaman. And because the snake was very long, the snake's head stuck out one end of the tunnel while his tail stuck out the other end.

The Great Shaman asked the snake why he was going to eat his friend the rat. The snake whipped his forked tongue from side to side and hissed, "Because it's in my nature."

The Great Shaman shook his head and with a sad smile pulled a pinch of salt from his pocket and sprinkled it *over the head of the snake. The snake instantly turned to stone; his head and tail above the ground, his body below the ground buried in the tunnel.*

So, whoever you are, your task is to locate the stone snake and follow these directions:

"Standing to the south of the snake, align yourself with the survivor of the fire and the viewer of the monuments, look to your right for the bite of the viper. Your treasure awaits within."

"Are you kidding? How in the heck are we supposed to figure that out?" exclaimed Amanda.

In a calmer voice, Mathew added, "Well, I guess the first thing we need to do is find the snake."

"And how do we do that?!"

"No idea. But given a little time and a little effort, I'm sure we can figure it out." Looking at Amanda, "Besides, what choice do we have? If we want to read the rest of the story, we need to find the snake."

Seeing that Amanda was frustrated, Mathew added, "We can do it. No problem."

Amanda quickly stood up and dusted off her backside, "Where are we going to find a snake? What kind of snake is it? Is it in Sedona or is it somewhere else?" Looking back at Mathew, "Why couldn't Scott just tell us where the rest of his dang story is?"

With a smile, Mathew said, "And I quote, *'if you earn the knowledge you will value it that much more.'*"

Amanda rolled her eyes, "Come on, we can figure this out later. It's already dark and we have a long way to drive before we get back to San Diego."

Sixty Days Later – Sixty Days After Discovering Scott and Susan's Story

As Amanda walked through the front door of their house, Mathew performed a jig, twirling and hopping in circles, as he waved a sheet of paper over his head,

"What's going on?" Amanda asked, stepping back to avoid Mathew's leg as he kicked the air. Reaching for Amanda's hands, Mathew pulled her into the center of the living room and continued his jig – turning Amanda in circles and jumping from one foot to the other.

Releasing Amanda's hands, Mathew raised the now crinkled sheet of paper above his head, "It's all ours. We are now the proud owners of a beautiful home in Sedona, Arizona."

Shortly after returning from their stopover visit in Sedona, where they found the mysterious story of Scott and Susan, Mathew and Amanda, after a few long discussions – Mathew was in love with the property, Amanda liked the property but wasn't sure if now was the right time – had made an offer on the property, it was accepted, and escrow closed today.

"That's great," Amanda said with a smile. "But there's a lot of work that needs to be done before we can actually live there – windows need replacing, new wood flooring in some areas, the ceiling nee . . ."

Mathew cut in, before Amanda had a chance to finish, "Yeah, yeah, there's stuff that needs to be done, but stop making it sound like a chore. It'll be fun." Grabbing Amanda around her waist, Mathew pulled her towards the couch, plopped down, and kissed her squarely on the lips, "We're homeowners!" he shouted.

Catching her breath, "I really am happy we own the property. It's such a beautiful place, the smells, the views, and the red rocks. It's wonderful."

"I think we should drive up this weekend," Mathew said excitedly. "We can camp out in the library and start fixing up the house."

Cautiously Amanda slowly said, "How's the sculpture coming for the restaurant – the *togetherness* piece?" Amanda knew that Mathew didn't like to be pushed, but she also knew he was having trouble with this commission – she was afraid he wasn't going to make the deadline. He had hardly started and had no idea what the design was going to look like. Typically by this time, Mathew would have had the sketch approved by the owners and be well into roughing out the stone.

Frustrated, Mathew replied, "It's getting there."

"Do you have the sketches done?" Trying to show some interest, Amanda added, "I'm anxious to see what the sculpture looks like?"

Sounding somewhat agitated, Mathew grunted, "Don't worry about it. I've got it under control. Have I ever missed a deadline?"

After a few silent moments, Amanda said in a low voice, "Have the owners signed off on the final design yet?"

After a few more heavy moments of silence, Mathew looked at Amanda and in a somewhat calmer voice said, "I know we need the money from the sculpture to help pay for the Sedona house. And yes, for some reason, I'm having difficulty getting started on this job. But I've got a few ideas floating around in my head and any day now I'll be able to come up with the design."

Amanda put her hand in Mathew's lap. "I don't mean to nag. I just want to make sure everything goes smoothly." After a pause, "Your clients just got married and they're opening a restaurant in La

Jolla and want a sculpture for the restaurant's atrium."

"Yes, I know," replied Mathew. "But I'm not even sure, at this stage, what they're really looking for. What in the heck does *togetherness* really mean?"

"How much time do you have? Is there anything I can do to help?"

"Only six weeks," mumbled Mathew. "I know it's short, but I can do it."

"Here's an idea," Amanda said. "I've got a ton of work to do this weekend for the charity auction at the hospital. How about this week I focus on the charity and you work on getting those *floating ideas* out of your head and onto a sketch pad so that the clients can sign off on the design. And next weekend we head up to Sedona and spend some time in our new home?"

Mathew smiled at Amanda, knowing she was probably right. "All right. This week we work, next weekend we play," repeated Mathew.

"Speaking of Sedona," said Amanda, "I've had zero luck trying to figure out where this stone snake is that we're supposed to find. Why this Scott . . . what's his last name . . . Morgan?"

"Montgomery, Scott Montgomery."

"Yeah, Montgomery. Why he made the clue so difficult, I'll never know. I bet Susan Cambell would have just told us where the rest of the story was."

"You remember Susan's last name, but not Scott's," Mathew smiled.

"Of course I do. There's something about her that I can relate to, like we're long lost cousins."

Laughing, Mathew added, "Maybe it's because you both have a tendency to get frustrated when you can't instantly come up with the solution?"

Surprised that Mathew would think that, Amanda said in a loud voice verging on frustration, "What're you talking about, I don't get frustrated!"

Mathew gave Amanda a hug. "You're probably right," he laughed.

"Well, what about you?" asked Amanda, pushing Mathew away. "Any luck on solving the clue?"

"Not much," replied Mathew, slouching down onto the couch, stretching out his legs, and interlocking his fingers behind his head. He closed his eyes and said, "I've spent hours on the computer scouring search engines for anything related to a snake or a rat or to friendship in Sedona and have come up with nothing. I've even plugged in *survivor of the fire* and *viewer of the monuments* and still got absolutely nothing."

"Maybe the snake's not in Sedona?" added Amanda.

"Maybe, but their story takes place in Sedona. It only makes sense that the clue would lead us to someplace in Sedona." After a short pause, "I even searched for any information I could find on Scott Montgomery and Susan Cambell. Unfortunately, they didn't keep many records back in the 40's and 50's, especially in a small town like Sedona. What I did find was very sketchy and even that was confusing." Taking in a slow breath, Mathew continued, "Scott was some kind of builder or designer or maybe his father was the builder or designer; there were a lot of contradictions in the documents. I also found a few old newspaper articles that covered the grand openings of a few buildings in Sedona that mentioned a Mr. Montgomery, but whether it was Scott or his father or what they did was unknown. And I found zero, absolutely nothing on Susan Cambell – as if she didn't exist."

Mathew turned towards Amanda and shrugged.

Amanda shrugged back.

One Week Later – Sixty-Seven Days After Discovering Scott and Susan's Story

Sitting beside Mathew on the front seat of their car, Amanda, in an attempt to block the sun from her eyes raised her right hand and squinted as she scanned the surrounding countryside covered in patches of low brush and dried grasses Focusing on his driving, as they crept along a dirt road full of ruts and overgrown grass, Mathew said, while vigilantly looking for the next pothole, "It appears like the last vehicle to have been on this road, if you can call this a road, was pulled by a horse."

"Where's the turnoff?" Amanda said, tired and frustrated with being jostled around from the bouncing of the car on the rough road. "And are you sure this is the right place? It seems far-fetched that Scott's clue would lead us all the way out here."

Turning the steering wheel to the left, guiding the front tires slowly around a large dip in the middle of the road, Mathew replied, "No I'm not sure. But it's the best I could come up with. I told you I've spent hours on the computer trying to figure out what the snake and rat story had to do with Sedona and it was all a waste of time. I found nothing. Eventually I called the real estate agent who we purchased our home from and asked if she knew of anything in Sedona that could possibly relate to a snake, a rat, or to friendship." Turning sharply to the right, Mathew pulled the front left tire out of a drainage rut and bumped back onto the less gnarled portion of the road. "She thought I was crazy, but she did mention an old overlook that no one goes to anymore. She thought the road might even have been washed out." Taking a quick look at Amanda, "No wise cracks, please." Looking back at the road, "We've made it this far so there's no way we're going to turn back now. If the car can't make it, we get out and walk. We're making it to the lookout point one way or the other."

"And remind me what this has to do with the clue?" Amanda asked, sounding somewhat grumpy.

"It's called *Friendship Point*. It's one of very few places in Sedona where you can see all the energy points - Boynton Canyon, Bell Rock, Airport Monument, and Cathedral Rock, all at the same time."

In a weary voice, Amanda said, "It's weak. Did the realtor mention anything about a snake or a rat?"

"No, she didn't remember anything about a rat or a snake. She said that she has never been up here, only that she remembered reading about *Friendship Point*."

Slumping down into her seat, Amanda quietly muttered, "This sounds shaky. I think we should've postponed our trip until we had more information. And you could have spent the extra time working on the sculpture."

Bringing the car to a sudden stop, Mathew turned to face his wife and said in a tone, verging on anger, "Amanda, we're already here. It's the best answer to the clue we have. Let's make the most of it and see what we can find." Taking a deep breath Mathew slowly exhaled, "And yes, I know, I'm still having trouble with the sculpture. Believe me, I know it. The owners have rejected my last three ideas, which I don't blame them for, because my ideas were crap. And yesterday before we left, the contractor for the restaurant phoned and told me they can't finish the roof until my sculpture is in place. They're going to use a crane to lower the sculpture down through the roof and they can't wait forever. And at the moment I don't have the remotest idea of what the sculpture will look like. So believe me, I know I'm having trouble with this commission."

Mathew took his foot off the brake pedal and little by little guided the car around a large rut. Amanda slid over next to Mathew, wrapped her hands around his upper arm - careful not to interfere with his driving and rested her head on his shoulder.

Mathew patted Amanda's thigh, before quickly returning his hand to the steering wheel just in time to maneuver around a few rocks. "You know I love you, Amanda," said Mathew. After a pause, "I'm hoping I'll get inspired by something I see along the way that I can use as the basis for the sculpture." After another pause, "At least I'm sure hoping I do."

*   *   *

"Am I good, or what?!" Mathew yelled to the sky, acting like he was king of the world.

"You're definitely good," mimicked Amanda.

Mathew, Amanda, and the car with a few extra superficial scratches had made it to the top of a small bluff that overlooked the town of Sedona. The road was not washed out, at least not much. On the edge of the bluff sat a stone snake curled around an old partially burned tree and what appeared to be a large metal flower. The body of the snake was partially buried as if it was going in and out through several underground tunnels. Wild grasses had taken over most of the stone snake, sprouting from every loose stone and grout joint. Wind-blown leaves had collected around its base.

Failing to see any sign of the rat, Amanda said, with a smile, "I guess the rat got away?"

"And look at this," Mathew said, standing next to the burned out tree trunk. "There's a plaque right here that warns people about the dangers of fire and says this tree survived the last large fire that passed through this area."

Nodding her head in delight, Amanda said, "The '*survivor of the fire*'. All right, now we're making progress. Okay, let's find the '*viewer of the monuments*.'"

Moving over to the large metal flower, Mathew said, "This is more than a flower, it's an observation scope of some sort. Look, there's a pipe sticking through the center of the flower." Reading the plaque next to the flower, Mathew slowly said, "It looks like, you're supposed to align the pointer, at the bottom of the flower stem, with a number engraved into the stone base. So if I align the pointer with the *number one* and then look through the pipe scope, I should be looking at Bell Rock."

Amanda rushed over, rotating the flower so that the pointer lined up with the *number one* and looked through the pipe. "Bell Rock. There it is, plain as day." Looking up, she turned the flower sculpture so that the pointer aligned with the number two. "Cathedral. I'm looking at Cathedral. Is that what the plaque says? Does the number two point to Cathedral?"

Continuing to read the plaque, Mathew looked up with a grin, "Number two is Cathedral."

Amanda raised her arms above her head and jumped in the air, "I think we've solved the clue! I can't believe it, we've found the clue!"

"And will you look at this," said Mathew. "It says right here that this structure was designed, built, and donated to the City of Sedona by Scott Montgomery."   Glancing up at Amanda, "We definitely have the right place."

"Okay Mathew, come on, read exactly what the clue says! Where are we supposed to stand?" Turning toward Mathew, Amanda added, "Where's the copy you made of the clue?"

"I'm already ahead of you," Mathew grinned, walking around to the south side of the stone snake, he pulled a folded piece of paper from his back pocket. "Okay, the clue says, '*Standing south of the snake, align yourself with the survivor of the fire and the viewer of the monuments.*'"

Amanda joined Mathew.   Visualizing an imaginary line between the old tree and the metal flower, Mathew and Amanda shuffled a few feet to their left.

Mathew read, "*Turn towards your right and look for the 'bite of the viper.'*"

Rotating her body to the right, Amanda questioned, "What

does a *viper bite* look like?"

"Maybe, it's the mouth of the actual stone snake? It's right here," suggested Mathew, as he took a few steps over to his left and patted the head of the snake. "This could be the *bite of the viper.*"

"But the head of the snake **is not** to the right of where we're standing – it's in front of us off to the left!" Quickly scanning the surface of the snake and the surrounding grass, Amanda said, "Mathew, you take a closer look at the snake and I'll search the grass next to the snake. Maybe the *bite of the viper* is hidden under a rock or covered with grass?"

Bending down onto his knees, Mathew made his way along the outside edge of the stone snake, inspecting each stone and mortar joint along the way. A minute and a-half later, Mathew quickly straightened up and shouted in an excited voice, "Amanda! Amanda come here! I think I found it."

Crawling around in the dry grass, Amanda promptly stood up, brushed the dirt and loose grass from her knees, and rushed over to Mathew.

"Look at this," Mathew said, pointing to a rock with two small holes carved in its side.

"What? Where?" Amanda cried, unable to figure out what Mathew had pointed at.

"The two holes!"

"What about the two holes?" probed Amanda.

"When a rattlesnake bites, it leaves two puncture holes in the skin . . . from its fangs." Mathew beamed, "*The bite of the viper!*"

"Oh-h-h-h-h-h," Amanda's replied. "I think you're right."

Smiling at Amanda, Mathew said, "Wife, the honor is all yours. Pull out the stone and let's see what we have."

Reaching forward Amanda firmly grasped the stone and tried to pull it from the body of the snake. It didn't budge - her fingers slipped off the smooth edges. Trying a second time, her fingers again slipped from the stone. "I can't get a clean hold. My fingers keep sliding off."

Holding up his hand, Mathew stuck out his first two fingers and curled them into the shape of fangs. "Make your fingers like this and put them in the two holes."

Amanda realizing how obvious that was, smiled to herself for not thinking of it herself, curled her fingers into the shape of fangs and then inserted them into the two holes on the face of the stone. She gently applied an upward pressure. The stone easily slipped out of its resting place.

Glancing over at Mathew, Amanda quickly bent over to take a look into the void left by the stone.

"E-E-E-E-E-E-K!" Amanda screamed and jumped back a good three feet. "There's the biggest black spider I've ever seen sitting in there!"

Slowly bending over, Mathew carefully peered into the stone cavity. Sitting on the lip of the small chamber was a very large black spider.

"What do we do?" Amanda impatiently asked.

Without saying a word, Mathew found a small stick and ever so slowly touched the front leg of the spider. The spider didn't move. Moving a little closer, Mathew nudged the spider a second time. Again the spider remained perfectly still.

Looking puzzled, Mathew said, more to himself than to Amanda, "Wait a minute. What's going on?"

Maneuvering the stick beyond the spider, Mathew flicked the spider out of the stone cavity onto the dry grass, where it landed upside down. Amanda shrieked and jumped back a few more feet. Mathew broke out laughing.

"What're you doing?" yelled Amanda, alarmed that Mathew would throw a spider in her direction. "And why're you laughing?"

In between laughs Mathew replied, somewhat pleased with

himself, "It's a rubber spider."

"A what?!" exclaimed Amanda.

Reaching over, Mathew picked up the spider and stretched out one of its legs before releasing it to snap back. "It's rubber," grinned Mathew.

"Yeah, very funny," said Amanda. "You know your sense of humor is very similar to Scott Montgomery's. Remember last Halloween when you rigged the doorbell so that a slimy hand would pop out of the mailbox, right in their face, whenever someone rang it?"

"Yeah, I remember, that was great."

With a smirk, Amanda shuck her head, "Exactly my point."

Mathew, not realizing what point Amanda was trying to make, gave her a quizzical look and said, "Forget about the spider, let's see what else is in the chamber."

"I'm not putting my hand in there!" Amanda cried out.

Picking up the stick, Mathew said, "No problem, I'll use this."

Pulling a flashlight out of his pack, Mathew aimed the light into the small rock chamber and saw a rolled–up leather pouch not more than a few inches inside the mouth. Snagging an edge of the pouch with the end of the stick, Mathew slowly dragged the pouch outward towards the entrance. Just as the stick was about to lose its grip, Amanda reached in with her thumb and forefinger and grabbed the pouch. Avoiding the possibility of coming into contact with any more spiders, she quickly tossed the pouch over to Mathew, "Here, you open it."

Brushing off the dust and a few spider webs, Mathew unrolled the leather pouch. On the front of the pouch, burned into the leather, was a small butterfly. Slowly and gently flipping back the cover, Mathew and Amanda saw an oilcloth wrapped package similar to the one they had found in the secret compartment of the desk.

"This is it!" exclaimed Mathew, smiling at Amanda.

"This is it," repeated Amanda smiling back.

Sitting in the dried brown grass, Mathew and Amanda settled back against the stone snake and began to read the handwritten pages.

PART TWO (Scott and Susan)

One Year Later: High School Seniors: Age Eighteen

For the past year, ever since Susan and I discovered our 'special place', the sandstone grotto, and lost our virginity to each other, neither of us have spoken much about the experience. To tell you the truth, it scared us a bit. Being in that spiritual place, feeling so close to each other and so connected to our surroundings was a very powerful experience. And then having to leave that magical place and return down the mountain back to school, back to homework, and back to our separate homes and separate lives was a very traumatic change. Plus we didn't fully understand what it all meant. The experience left us a bit *shell shocked*.

Occasionally Susan would turn to face me from across the classroom or from across the lunch yard or as we walked arm in arm across town, she'd look up into my eyes and give me this faraway look; the same relaxed faraway look she had while we lay on the grass gazing up at the soft blue sky through the swaying leaves of the majestic sycamore in the sandstone grotto – this *knowing look* that let me know that we had something special and that she hadn't forgotten about the sandstone grotto, *our 'special place'*. And I would return with my own knowing look and smile back at her. It would only last a moment or two, then she or I would be distracted and look away and then the spell was broken and we would return to whatever it was we were doing. Other than that, we had more or less avoided the subject and never returned to the grotto.

As far as our virginity, we were both happy that we had lost it to each other in such a special place in such a special way. And, I kind of hoped we could give it a few more tries, but Susan reminded me that she had always wanted to wait until after we were married, and just because she slipped once didn't mean that she had changed her mind on the subject. Reluctantly, I respected her wishes.

*   *   *

Susan and I, with Raymond James between us, leisurely rumbled along a well-worn dirt road lined with sage, cactus, and ocotillo in my old truck in need of paint and a little loving care, creating a small cloud of dust slowly rising in our wake.

"Why did you want to go out to *Sage Point?*" I asked.

Sage Point was located just outside Sedona on the edge of a butte overlooking the desert to the west. It's a great place to watch the long shadows and muted colors of the setting sun across the desert floor.

"I don't know." Susan said, as she shrugged her shoulders and then added, "I guess, I'm a little sad. This is our senior year of high school. We only have a week left of school and then everything changes. No more driving to school together, no more eating together with friends at lunch, no more doing homework together, no more school together, and worst of all . . . " Reaching over with both hands. Susan scratched the loose skin below Raymond James' ears and gave him a kiss on the forehead. "No more Raymond James." Raymond James returned the kiss with a quick lick to her cheek. "This is what I've been doing since I was eight years old and now it's all going to change." After a moment she added, "I suppose I'm a little scared that I'm going to lose everything I have."

I placed my arm around Susan's shoulders and pulled her in close. Raymond James didn't seem to mind being squashed between us.

We drove quietly along the dirt road for another few minutes until we reached *Sage Point*. The sun had an hour left before reaching the horizon and the sharp crisp close-in view of the cactus, shrubs, and lots of emptiness contrasted beautifully with the fuzziness of the distant mountains – it was gorgeous.

Leaning over I kissed the top of Susan's head and tenderly said, "I know it can be a little scary leaving behind things you've grown to care for. But not everything will change." After a moment, I smiled and said, "I'll still have this fine old truck." Susan elbowed me in the ribs. "Also," I added with a chuckle, "you'll only be a few hours away in Flagstaff. Raymond James and I will be visiting you at college and you'll be coming home on the weekends. And our friends will still be here. Look at it as a promotion. You've performed so well in high school that you're being promoted to college." Looking into Susan's green eyes, I smiled, "You should be happy. You should be looking forward to all the new experiences you're going to have. And I'll always be here for you. If you ever need anything, just ask." I folded my arms around Susan and softly squeezed.

*   *   *

After gradation Susan had been accepted to Northern Arizona University in Flagstaff and was planning to leave in the fall. She had wanted us to travel together after high school, to see the world and to give a little something of ourselves back to others. Her mother, however, insisted that Susan attend an Ivy League college back east before going off on, and I quote, "Any foolish adventures." As a compromise, Susan agreed to attend Northern Arizona University, to major in education and to become a teacher.

With Susan away at college, I had decided to work with my dad full time; he was swamped and I could use the money. After Susan's four years of college, we talked about marriage. We both knew it was going to happen, but neither of us was in any hurry. We were very happy with the way things were. I had also entertained the idea of attending an architectural program at a place in Arizona called *Taliesin West*. It was run by a guy named Frank Lloyd Wright. I'd heard some good things about him, the way he used the natural material of the site to build with and the way his buildings blended into their surroundings. I had always enjoyed the process of creating and building structures and being outdoors among the canyons, and streams, and red rocks was like a second home to me. So going to *Taliesin West* seemed like a good fit. But for now my dad needed the help and I needed the cash; maybe in a year or two.

*   *   *

Sitting in the front seat of my old truck, Susan and I quietly stared out across the desert. Raymond James head rested on Susan's lap. "Are you and Maria ready for the prom?" I quietly asked.

Our senior prom was in four days, the last day of school. Susan and Maria had been going crazy in their preparations for the prom; looking through magazines at all the dresses and different types of hairstyles, going to the drugstore to try out the various eye shadows and lipsticks and foundations and whatever else they put on their faces, visiting shoe stores to see the latest styles, and making day trips to Flagstaff and Phoenix to look at . . . who knows what?

Perking up at the mention of the prom, Susan smiled and said, "We're ready." Sitting up a little straighter, she looked over at me, "Maria and I are planning to meet at my house in the afternoon, have lunch, play a few games, and then we'll get ready. My mother has hired a beautician from Flagstaff to come over and do our nails, apply our makeup, and give each of us a fantastic *Ava Gardner*."

"It sounds as if this beautician will be doing everything," I laughed, "All you'll have to do is sit there and relax." Raising my eyebrows into a questioning look, "An *Ava Gardner*?" I asked.

"Yeah. Don't tell me you've never heard of an *Ava Gardner*. It's all the rage. It's the latest in hairstyles, and every girl at the prom is going to have one. It's the hairstyle that Ava Gardner wears – the hair is all rolled up into a bun on the back of your head. And for you . . ." Susan gave me a sly look, "I'm going to add a few pieces of sage mixed into the bun so that when we're dancing close you can smell the sage. I know how you love the smell of the desert."

"You're the greatest," I said kissing her on the tip of her nose. "But, how are you going to manage to get into your dress and shoes all by yourself? Is the beautician going to help you with that as well, she seems to be doing everything else?"

"Very funny," giggled Susan. "All I can say is that you better be looking your very best." Pausing, she added, "Have you picked up your suit?"

"Of course."

"And have you arranged to borrow William's Cadillac Eldorado?"

William was my dad's friend who passed on to us the directions to the sandstone grotto and had given Raymond James to me. William loved big fast cars and had a ten year old Cadillac, with a rebuilt engine and a new shiny red paint job. "Yes, I have."

"And you're picking me up at six o'clock sharp?"

"Yes," I said, and then added, "Is the beautician coming with us?"

With a frown, Susan looked at me, "Okay, enough, give it a rest!" And then punched me in the arm. "Okay, let's go. And let me drive. I've got to practice my driving before I go to Flagstaff."

Susan's college roommate had a new *Ford Crestline Skyliner* – a graduation present from her father. The roommate offered to share the car with Susan for trips around Flagstaff, as long as Susan could learn to drive a stick shift. For the last few weeks Susan has been practicing on my old truck, getting a feel for driving with a stick.

Exchanging places, Susan sat behind the steering wheel, turned the key to the engine and put the gear shift into reverse, slowly making a very nice three-point turn, especially for someone that knew very little about using a clutch.

"Good job," I said as I patted Raymond James, still sitting between us, on his shoulders.

Raymond James, encouraged Susan with a small bark of approval.

At the bottom of the butte, Susan immediately turned left at the first fork in the dirt road.

"Wait . . . wait a minute. Where're you going?!" I shouted, surprised that Susan had turned left.

Stomping on the brake pedal, Susan brought us to an abrupt stop; or almost to a stop, as the engine jerked the truck forward and then died.

To keep from slipping forward, I quickly extended my arms outward and grabbed the dashboard. Raymond James barked and slid off the seat into the passenger side foot well – his nails, trying to gain traction, scratched along the worn cloth seat covers.

Susan turned to look at us, smiled, and said, "Whoops!"

Raymond James instantly scrambled back onto the seat between us and gave Susan a quick lick on the skin of her exposed shoulder. Susan rubbed Raymond James all over and whispered into his ear, "Sorry, pal. I'm still getting used to driving this thing."

I said, "This road leads out into the desert. The other road will take us back into town."

"Oh," replied Susan with no concern whatsoever at having made a wrong turn. She backed the truck up and headed down the correct dirt road.

"I have an idea," I said, looking at Susan as she concentrated on shifting gears, "when you're in Flagstaff and you want to go somewhere, whatever direction you think you should take, take the opposite direction."

Laughing, Susan said, "I'm going to miss seeing you every day."

*   *   *

It's amazing what a guy will do for a girl. Dances and crowds were not on my list of top ten things I liked to do. Susan, on the other hand, loved anything associated with music – singing, playing instruments (she played the piano and guitar), and of course, dancing. I'd been able to avoid most school dances and church socials by working late with my dad or by not feeling *my best* at opportune times. But the senior prom was important to Susan, something she'd remember for the rest of her life, so I made an effort to do my part.

First off, I learned to dance. Oh, I'd danced with Susan before, shuffling my feet and counting, *one, and two, and three, and four* as we fumbled our way through a turn. But at the prom I wanted to dazzle her with my footwork, not step on her toes. Mrs. Clark, who worked at the post office, taught me the finer points of gliding across the dance room floor; not just the standard dance moves like the foxtrot and waltz, but also some of Susan's favorites: the Lindy Hop and the Swing.

Mrs. Clark was my dad's friend who lived in San Francisco before coming to Sedona. A while back she lost her husband to pneumonia. She never cared much for the big city, so after her husband passed on she moved to Sedona. Mrs. Clark and my dad saw each other from time to time. My father never remarried, he said he was blessed to have had the perfect mate and he was satisfied with that. But, that didn't stop him from having his share of female friends and attending his share of dinners, movies, and church dances. More than a few times I woke up to breakfast and the smell of perfume.

I also made Susan a special corsage. I could have bought her a corsage of lilies and orchids that looked like all the other corsages at the prom but I wanted something unique. I went out and picked the flowers from a small shaded canyon at the foot of Cathedral Rock. Susan and I had discovered the canyon while hiking the south trail. We parked at a small turnout about three quarters of a mile past the more heavily used main trail that headed up the west face of Cathedral and hiked the almost non-existent, seriously overgrown portion of the south trail that headed east. When the trail veered away from Cathedral Rock towards Phoenix, we headed north in the direction of a sandstone rock in the shape of a *spool of thread*. Just behind the spool was the opening into a small canyon. The canyon was full of beautiful suncups, prairie fires, lupine, and many other flowering plants. The smells were heavenly and it became one of our favorite places. It wasn't until later I remembered that I had been to the canyon many years before with my dad. I was eight or nine at the time and he had showed me a sandstone wall full of pictographs – symbols depicting the sun and the moon and floods and all sorts of animals. There were even stories about great hunts and stories showing years with very little rain.

My corsage for Susan consisted mainly of the muted red prairie fires and the bright yellow suncups. I had picked them in the shade of the canyon walls and then added a touch of dusty-green sage to match the smell of sage Susan was going to put in her . . . *Ava Gardner*. I arranged the flowers into something resembling a corsage. Mrs. Clark said it was the loveliest corsage she had ever seen.

I'd also washed and waxed the Cadillac Eldorado we were borrowing from William and finally I had picked up my dad's best suit, actually his only suit, from the seamstress who'd altered it just a little so that it would fit my longer legs.

Like I said, it's amazing what a guy will do for a girl.

Four Days Later - The Night of the Senior Prom: Age Eighteen

The big night of the senior prom had arrived. I hadn't seen Susan all day; she and her friend Maria had been preening and prancing their way through the day as they got ready for the big night. I felt good sitting behind the wheel of the smooth riding Eldorado – my arm out the window and Buddy Holly playing on the radio. Raymond James was lying in the back seat with a black tuxedo bow tie wrapped around his neck, like a ribbon on a gift. My dad's suit jacket was tight around my shoulders, but I figured I could take it off once we got to the auditorium. My corsage for Susan was patiently resting next to me on the front seat.

Susan lived with her mother in a large wooden ranch house that sat low to the ground and had a wide sweeping roof supported by a colonnade of oak tree trunks that wrapped around the house. The property consisted of one hundred and forty acres of rolling hills covered in majestic oaks and sycamores. The property on the back side of the house swept gently down to the shores of Oak Creek.

As I pulled onto the curved gravel driveway leading up to Susan's house, Raymond James started to whine and after a few moments stood up in the back seat and clawed at the rear side window closest to the house.

Raymond James didn't normally whine so I figured something was up. "What is it Raymond James?" I asked with concern as I leaned over the back of the front seat to look at him. He barked and continued to paw at the window, as if he was trying to get out of the car.

The air was dead still and peering through the trees I could see there wasn't a single light on in the house. "What is it Raymond James?" I repeated.

Quickly pulling up to the front porch, I abruptly brought the Cadillac to a rough stop and pushed open the driver's side door – the corsage next to me on the front seat slid forward, fell off the seat and landed face down in the passenger side foot well.

Raymond James immediately made an attempt to escape the back seat. I took hold of his collar and led him back into the car as I slammed the car door shut. Running up the wide sweeping steps I banged on the front door and waited . . . there was no response. From behind me I could hear Raymond James barking inside the car. I reached for the door knob, gave it a twist, and pushed inward. The door opened easily. Quickly stepping into the front entry, the house completely dark, I hollered, "Mrs. Cambell, Susan are you here?!" No one responded.

From outside I heard a panicked voice shout, "Mr. Scott, Mr. Scott. Mrs. Cambell is at the hospital!"

Running back out through the front door and down to the gravel driveway, I saw their housekeeper rushing towards me from around the far corner of the house. I hollered back, "Mrs. Gonzalez, what are you talking about? Is Susan hurt and is she in the hospital? What happened?"

Mrs. Gonzalez lived in a small house in the back with her husband. She took care of the housekeeping chores and her husband took care of the grounds.

"No! No! Mr. Scott! Miss Susan is not in the hospital, her mother is." Mrs. Gonzalez was excited, out of breath, and talking very fast.

"Wait a minute, slow down Mrs. Gonzalez." Taking a deep breath and letting it out, I said, "Mrs. Cambell is hurt and is in the hospital?"

"Yes! Yes!"

"And Susan isn't hurt? She's okay?"

"Yes! Yes! And the police came and took Miss Susan to the hospital to be with Mrs. Cambell."

Realizing that Susan wasn't injured, I relaxed a little. "What happened to Mrs. Cambell?"

"She was in a bad auto accident. The police said a big truck hit her from behind."

Wanting to reach Susan and to find out how Mrs. Cambell was doing, I rushed over to the Cadillac and shouted back to Mrs. Gonzalez, "Which hospital, the big one in Phoenix?"

"Mr. Scott, I don't know, maybe Sedona."

I jumped into the front seat as Mrs. Gonzalez ran over to my side of the car and said, "My husband and I are so worried about Mrs. Cambell. Please let us know if everything is okay."

With Raymond James barking and nervously prancing around the passenger side front seat, I reached out the Cadillac window, locked hands with Mrs. Gonzalez, looked her in the eyes and nodded, "As soon as I find out anything I'll let you know."

*   *   *

I sailed down the highway, it was pitch dark outside, not another car in sight. All I saw was the glow of my headlights shining thirty feet down the road in front of me. I was going close to eighty miles per hour, headed south towards St. Frances Memorial Hospital in Phoenix. Raymond James sat next to me in the front seat. He was shaking a bit and whining from time to time, but his eyes were alert and focused. He was helping me watch the road and would let out with a small yelp whenever he saw anything move at the front edge of the lights – Raymond James saw far better than I could in the dark.

Raymond James was nervous and I could tell he felt

helpless - knowing something was wrong, but not knowing what. And I'm sure he wondered, where Susan was - Susan was typically always with us! I talked to him in a calming voice and rubbed his head, but nothing seemed to help.

It would typically take me a little over four hours to make the trip to Phoenix. I hoped to make it in half that time. If the police tried to pull me over, I wasn't going to stop until I reached the hospital.

Before heading out towards Phoenix, I had stopped by the small clinic in Sedona and the nurse told me that the ambulance had arrived with Mrs. Cambell, but other than trying to stop the bleeding there wasn't much they could do. After a short stop to pick up a few supplies, the ambulance immediately took off towards Phoenix. The nurse told me that Susan was with her mother in the ambulance and that the clinic had phoned ahead and informed St. Frances Memorial that the ambulance was on its way. Just before I left, I asked the nurse how Mrs. Cambell was and she gave me a sad look, closed her eyes, and shook her head.

*   *   *

With an effort, I forcefully held Raymond James in the car as I closed the car door. He was not happy as he barked and patrolled the inside of the car trying to find a way out.

Rushing towards the entry to the emergency ward of St. Francis Memorial, I pushed open the doors and immediately headed for the admitting desk.

Out of breath, I quickly asked, "There was an auto

accident. A Mrs. Cambell was rushed here from Sedona. How is she doing? And her daughter Susan came with her. Is she here?'"

Calmly staring back at me, as if she was used to dealing with distressed people, she gave me a sympathetic look and pointed over my right shoulder to the corner of the waiting room.

Turning my head to follow the direction of her finger, I saw Susan sitting in the corner . . . quietly crying. She wore a pale green, full-length silk gown with polished open-toed black shoes. She didn't have on much makeup, but the little mascara she did have was streaking down her cheeks. A few strands of hair from her *Ava Gardner* had fallen loose and were dangling over the left front side of her face. On her left sleeve was a bright red smear of blood.

I immediately hurried over to Susan, bent down, and wrapped my arms around her. Crying into my chest, Susan whimpered, "There was so much blood." A few hard sobs later, "And the doctors had such a hard time stopping all the bleeding. There was so much blood."

Holding her tightly, I softly kissed the top of her head. Smelling a hint of sage in her hair, I whispered, "I'm here, Susan. Whatever you need . . ."

I was immediately interrupted by the clatter of hard rubber tires wobbling across the linoleum floor as a gurney pushed by two male attendants dressed in white, shouting to each other, rushed by us and out the side door. A tall doctor, dressed in green surgical scrubs, rushed over to us and gently but firmly pulled Susan up from her chair and away from my embrace as he said, "We need to fly your mother to All Saints Hospital in Los Angeles - they are far better equipped to deal with your mother's injuries. We've obtained a helicopter from the Navajo Army Depot and we're rushing your mother out right now." Taking hold of Susan's hand, the doctor guided Susan past me and out the side door as they followed the other doctors, nurses, and orderlies to the waiting helicopter.

Just as the doors were about to swing closed, I rushed over, grasped the edge of the door, and slipped through. Fifty feet away, I saw one of the orderlies that was pushing the gurney, reach up and grab a corner of the blanket covering Mrs. Cambell and in an effort to keep the blanket from blowing away, quickly pulled it tight and wedged it into the corner of the steel frame of the gurney. The area beneath the spinning blades of the helicopter had turned into a small windstorm. Eventually a nurse rushed over to help hold down the blanket as the two men lifted the gurney, folded under the legs, and slid Mrs. Cambell into the open bay of the helicopter. Two doctors, a few nurses, and a bunch of equipment were all piled in. And finally, one of the doctors already sitting in the helicopter pointed towards Susan. An orderly still on the ground quickly lifted Susan up into the seat next to the doctor. The ground crew rushed in and slammed the sliding helicopter door shut. The remaining hospital personnel were ushered back and a man wearing a set of headphones shouted something to the pilot. Immediately the blades began to gain speed.

The whole scene was very confusing: people running back

and forth from the hospital to the helicopter, everyone shouting trying to be heard, the wind from the blades causing havoc, and above it all raining down on us was the high pitched whine of the engines.

But none of this confusion penetrated my awareness. I was focused on Susan – seeing what she was doing, where she was going, and wanting to make sure she was all right. The last thing I saw, as the helicopter slowly lifted off the landing strip and tilted west towards Los Angeles, was Susan staring at me out the side window of the helicopter - the palms of her hands pressed tightly against the glass, strands of her hair dangling across her face, her pale green dress muted by the dirty glass of the helicopter's window, and the smear of blood on her left shoulder. But what I remember most was the all-is-lost look on Susan's face – her pale white skin tone; the downward tilt of the outside edges of her mouth; the confused drooping expression on her forehead; and for the first time the deep green shine in her eyes, the shine that I had noticed the first time I had met her in her mother's barn at the age of eight, the shine that had always brightened my day, my life . . . had disappeared.

I stood outside the side door of the hospital leaning against the rough textured stucco wall for a long time. I heard Raymond James barking and whining in the distance.

I couldn't get the all-is-lost look on Susan's face out of my head. I wanted to be with Susan, to hold her, to do what I could to help, to do what I could to bring the light back into her green eyes. I felt frustrated and helpless and a little scared.

At some point in the early morning hours, I made my way

over to William's Cadillac and to Raymond James. Sliding into the front seat, Raymond James knew something wasn't right - he could sense my sadness. Immediately he stopped barking, placed his front paws on my lap - his tuxedo bowtie upside down but still round his neck - and looked up at me with the saddest dark eyes I had ever seen; eyes that were pleading, eyes that were asking . . . where's our Susan? I half attempted a smile but failed as I gently rubbed between his ears.

We slowly headed back to Sedona. The clock on the dashboard read a little past three in the morning. Below Raymond James in the passenger side foot well rested a small box containing my home made corsage of prairie fires, suncups, and sage. I wondered if Susan would ever smell the sage or feel the softness of the suncups against her skin.

End of Part Two

"That's the last page," whispered Mathew, "The end of Part Two."

Amanda, lying against the stone snake, her head tilted back resting on her folded up sweatshirt, felt warmed by the afternoon sun, now straight overhead. She was relaxed and focused on Mathew's every word as he read the story. Upon hearing Mathew say, "That's the last page," she quickly opened her eyes and bolted upright. "What a horrible place to end the story – right in the middle of having Susan fly off into the night. This Scott Montgomery definitely has a mean streak in him, leaving us hanging like that." Exasperated, Amanda took in a breath and on the exhale, said, "Hey, here's an idea. We have the rest of today and tomorrow morning before we need to head back to San Diego. Maybe we can solve the next clue before we leave?"

"It's worth a try," replied Mathew, reaching for the last sheet laying in the bottom of the folded up oilcloth.

C l u e   No.   T w o

Congratulations, you have made it this far. Hope you haven't lost interest because the best is yet to come. By the way, how'd you like the spider?"

Looking up, Mathew smiled at Amanda. Amanda frowned and quickly said, "Keep reading."

Recognize this set of petroglyphs? They tell the friendship story between the snake and the rat and the Great Shaman - I suspect much more precisely than I told it to you.

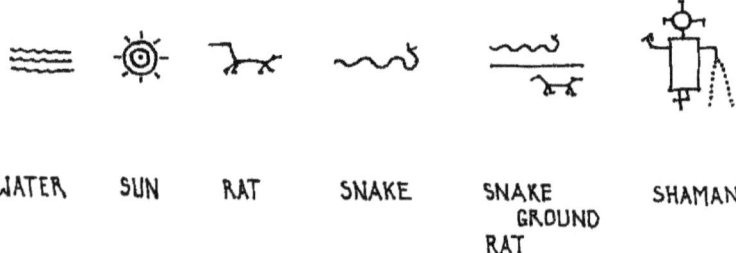

WATER   SUN   RAT   SNAKE   SNAKE GROUND RAT   SHAMAN

My dad and I hiked to these petroglyphs one Sunday morning a long time ago. While eating lunch in the shade of the petroglyphs, my dad passed the story on to me and I've passed it on to you.

I'm sure you know what petroglyphs are, but playing the role of my dad and just to refresh your memory – petroglyphs are carvings or paintings made on rocks by ancient civilizations. Most of the ones I've seen around Sedona are 'scraped' petroglyphs rather than painted or carved. Over the centuries the rains running down the sides of the sandstone cliffs leached out the iron and magnesium. This iron and magnesium created a thin dark layer of rust, similar to rusting metal, on the face of the cliffs. This layer of rust is called *desert varnish* and is usually a dark brown or black. The creator of the petroglyphs would then scrape off or peck off the desert varnish exposing the lighter sandstone below, hence the 'scraping' method of petroglyphs. The petroglyphs were usually created to mark special events in the lives of the People – great hunts, spiritual ceremonies, the moon and the sun marking the harvest and hunting seasons.

I'm not sure who created these petroglyphs conveying the friendship story – whether it was the early tribes of the Sinaqua People, meaning the People Without Water who were in the Sedona area around 1000AD or the later tribes of the Wipukepa People, also known as the Mohave Apache meaning the *People of the Red Rock* who first appeared around 1800AD, or some teenagers on a Friday night thinking it was romantic to scratch the names of their girlfriends in the rock.

Did I explain it okay dad?

I do know, however, that below these petroglyphs, close to the ground and carved in the red stone, is a small butterfly. I carved the butterfly, and just below it is the next segment of Susan's and my story.

Your task is to solve the puzzle below, locate the petroglyphs, my butterfly, and the story. I will tell you that the petroglyphs are in plain sight below a large overhang of red sandstone about four feet off the ground.

The rest is up to you. Best of luck.
Scott Montgomery

```
10    28 13 26   16  4     11 29 18
 I  -  R  O  T  -  I  N  -  M  U  D


27 23 9  7 20 19 6 24 21 34
 B  A  R  G  A  I  N  I  N  G


33 8 22 12 35 31 15 25 32 5 2 3 17 1 14 30
 A  P  P  R  E  H  E  N  S  I  V  E  N  E  S  S
```

"You've got to be kidding," exclaimed Amanda. *"I ROT IN MUD, BARGAINING, APPREHENSIVENESS.* What the heck does that mean? And what do the numbers mean? This is crazy; just a bunch of gobbledygook."

Still relaxing back against the stone snake Mathew laughed, "Amanda we can do this. Scavenger hunts are fun."

"Haa! Fun for you and for this Scott character. You two are like two peas in a pod. But me, I like it when things are handed to me on a silver platter; forget about having to work for them. Scott and his father had it all wrong."

Standing up, Mathew put his arm around Amanda's shoulders and led her towards the parked car. "I think solving this clue is going to take some time." Giving Amanda a squeeze, "Let's go work on the house."

Five Weeks Later - After Discovering The Rat And The Snake In Sedona

Dressed up in their finest attire, Mathew and Amanda stood arm in arm off to the side in the back corner of the atrium of the new restaurant, *TOGETHERNESS*. They were observing the reactions of the crowd meandering past Mathew's latest sculpture. It was the grand opening of the restaurant and the unveiling of his sculpture. The sculpture sat directly in the middle of the atrium, highlighted by several strategically placed hidden spotlights. Most of the crowd stopped to give the sculpture a second look and a few pointed at and discussed various aspects of the sculpture in more detail.

"Good job, husband," smiled Amanda as she pulled herself a little tighter into Mathew's side. "I never had any doubt that you would make the deadline."

Mathew glanced down at Amanda, and with a crooked smile, "Never any doubts? . . . Haa!"

"Well, maybe just a few little ones."

The sculpture stood over eight feet tall but was no more than a couple feet in diameter and was carved from pure white marble imported from Italy. The stone, *Carrara Marble*, was brought in from a quarry in Carrara, a town nestled in the Alps of northern Tuscany. It was from the same quarry as the stone used by Michelangelo to carve the famous statue of *David* - the owners of the restaurant spared no expense. When you first glanced at the sculpture it looked somewhat like an abstract ballerina with her arms outstretched over her head. But in actuality it was two tall thin undulating cylinders, about ten inches in diameter, extending from the base of the sculpture to its top. At the base, the two cylinders started as separate objects - about three feet apart. But as your eyes traveled up from the base, the two cylinders grew closer and closer together, until about eighteen inches up the two cylinders joined. A little further up, the cylinders began to wrap around each other, and then at the top they intertwined into one cylinder as if the two had become one. At the very top, four arm-like appendages stretched out, up, and around until they joined above the top of the sculpture, like the arms of a ballerina. But, if you looked close you'd see a faint outline of a leg and then maybe you'd see a hip and then a breast and eventually at the top perhaps there were two heads. And if you were really observant you'd realize the two cylinders were actually two humans who started off as separate beings and over time had grown together as one. The spotlights reflecting off the white marble added to the mystical glow of the statue.

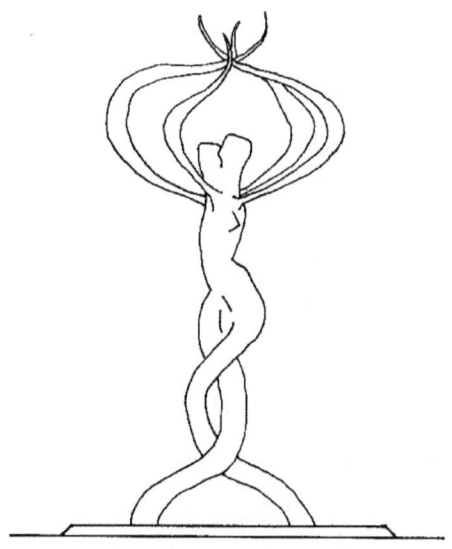

Giving Mathew's arm a little squeeze, Amanda said, "I think it's absolutely the best piece you've ever created."

"I owe it all to Sedona," replied Mathew. "When we left the stone snake at Friendship Point . . . I . . . I felt . . . I don't know, just . . . energized with inspiration." Thinking back on the trip, Mathew added, "It all came to me on our drive home. An idea developed in my head, I played with it as we drove, adding a little here, subtracting a little there, turned it this way and that way in my head, and by the time we reached San Diego, I knew I had the design."

"You're the best, husband."

"Mathew, you've done an outstanding job." Mathew heard a deep voice from behind him as he felt a hand slide onto his shoulder, "It's wonderful. We couldn't have asked for more."

Turning, Mathew and Amanda smiled at the owners of the new restaurant. Mathew, shaking the owner's hand, said, "Thanks, Mr. Southcott. I appreciate the nice words and nice to see you again, Mrs. Southcott." After a short pause, Mathew added, "Great dress Mrs. Southcott."

Giving Mathew a smile for his compliment, Mrs. Southcott turned to look at the sculpture. "Mathew, we asked you to come up with something that represented *togetherness*, which is why we named the restaurant, *TOGETHERNESS,* and I think you've hit the nail right on the head. I get goose bumps every time I look at it."

"You're more than generous," replied Mathew.

Turning his head towards the restaurant door, Mr. Southcott said, "I see a few guests we need to thank for their support." Mr. Southcott shook Mathew's hand and gave Amanda a quick hug. "Again, Mathew thanks for everything, great job." Halfway to the busy entrance, Mr. Southcott turned back to Mathew and Amanda, "When you're ready, come on in, dinner is on us."

Mathew smiled and waved back, "Thanks."

After the Southcott's disappeared through the dining room doors, Mathew leaned into Amanda and said, "I'm ready to leave. How about you?" After a pause, "Too many people for my taste."

Amanda smiled and nodded her approval, "Suits me fine."

*　　　*　　　*

Pulling out of the restaurant's parking lot, Mathew pointed their car in the direction of home, and said with a bit of cheer in his voice, "Six more days and we're off to Sedona for our three-week holiday!"

"What about the clue from Scott and Susan's story? We haven't solved it yet," added Amanda.

"Yes we have," Mathew swiftly replied. "Remember I mentioned it to you a few nights ago when you walked into the house after work. You were completely wasted. It was the day all those people from the bus crash ended up in your emergency ward."

"Did it seem like I was paying attention when you told me about the solution to the clue?"

Thinking back, Mathew said, "Well, you were awfully quiet. And you didn't ask your usual questions. And you did ask me to repeat myself a few times."

"Well, there you go, I was probably half asleep," Amanda said, shaking her head. "Tell me again what the solution to the clue is and how you figured it out?"

"*EVENING PRIMROSE, INDIAN PAINTBRUSH, SAGE,*" Mathew glanced at Amanda and then quickly back at the road in front of him.

"Oh yeah, now it's coming back to me," responded Amanda repeating the clue softly to herself. "Evening Primrose, Indian Paintbrush, and Sage. And how'd you figure that out?"

"It was easy. It was an anagram," exclaimed Mathew. "You know, you take the letters from a few words and scramble them all up."

Amanda, unconvinced that Mathew could figure this out on his own, "There were a lot of letters, how'd you figure it out?"

"Like I said, it was easy. I plugged all the letters into an anagram program I found online, hit a key and, presto change-o, out came the answer." Shaking his head, "There's no way I could have figured it out on my own, there were just too many letters."

Nodding her head, Amanda thought about the clue a few moments longer, "How'd Scott Montgomery expect someone to figure it out? They didn't have computers back then?"

"Because of the numbers," Mathew quickly answered. "Remember each letter had a number directly above it. If you arranged the numbers along with their accompanying letters in sequence – *1,2,3,4* . . . etc., the letters would spell - *Evening Primrose, Indian Paintbrush, Sage*." Feeling good Mathew added, "You wouldn't need a computer if you figured out the numbers."

"So-o-o-o-o instead of figuring out the number sequence first, which would then give you the words, you figured out the words first, and then the numbers?" Smiling at Mathew, Amanda continued, "You figured it out backwards!"

"What can I say, when you're good, you're good," beamed Mathew. "Scott Montgomery would have never thought that was possible. Man, would he be impressed with what computers can do."

"Okay, smart guy," Amanda said punching him in the arm, "How does Evening Primrose, Indian Paintbrush, and Sage get us any closer to finding the next installment of the story?"

"Th-a-a-a-a-t I haven't quite figured out yet," Mathew answered, nudging Amanda back. "Evening Primrose, Indian Paintbrush, and Sage are all plants that grow around Sedona. But that's the problem; they grow **all around** Sedona. What specific area we're supposed to search is still unknown."

Leaning back in the passenger seat of their car, Amanda mumbled, "Well, you have six days to figure it out." Closing her eyes she said, "Let me know when we get home."

Seven Days Later

"Is this the right turnout?" asked Mathew, turning his head

from right to left, trying to figure out if they'd missed the turnout or if it was still ahead of them.

"This has got to be it," responded Amanda. "I don't see anything else that looks remotely like a turnout." Looking to the left she added, "And there's Cathedral Rock, just like the story said."

*   *   *

Last night Mathew and Amanda had arrived in Sedona and spent the night in sleeping bags on the floor of their new house. They decided to spend the first part of their three-week vacation trying to solve the mystery of Scott and Susan before jumping head first into the deep end of home repairs.

Evening Primrose, Indian Paintbrush, Sage... Even though Mathew was confident he could figure out how these words related to finding the next part of the story, it was actually Amanda who came up with the solution. Amanda had plugged each of the three plants into Google and read as much as she could about each of them. She discovered that the common name for the *Evening Primrose* was *Suncups*. And the common name for the *Indian Paintbrush* was *Prairie Fire*. She remembered that Scott Montgomery had created a corsage for Susan Cambell for their senior prom from Suncups, Prairie Fires, and Sage. And while listening to Mathew read the story for the first time, Amanda had wondered why Scott had gone into so much detail in describing the location of the small canyon where he had picked the flowers. And now she knew . . . he was giving directions to the next part of his and Susan's story.

*   *   *

Pulling their car off to the side of the old dirt road, Mathew said with some uncertainty, "We're supposed to park in a turnout somewhere around here. But, can you really call this a turnout? It's more like the road has just widened out a bit."

"I don't see anything else. Let's park and give it a try," replied Amanda.

Grabbing the backpack from the rear seat, Mathew and Amanda started off along the almost nonexistent trail heading east.

Forty-five minutes later, somewhat winded and with a sheen of perspiration sparkling on her forehead, Amanda asked, "Is this where we leave the trail? Should we turn here?" Looking up at the cloudless blue sky, she pulled a bottle of water from her pack, then added, "It's going to be a hot one."

Looking further up the trail, Mathew uttered, "I'm not sure. Maybe we should continue a little further along the trail before we head north?"

"The story says," Amanda raised the water bottle to her lips and took a few gulps before continuing. "That we turn north when the trail veers south away from Cathedral. And the trail is definitely veering south away from Cathedral. This means, we go off the trail to the north."

Shading the sun from his eyes, Mathew said, "Yeah, but it looks so empty out there." Scanning the distant rock formations, "Wait . . . wait a minute. Look over there." Pointing toward the base of Cathedral Rock, "Doesn't that boulder look a lot like a *spool of thread?*"

Squinting to see what Mathew was pointing at, Amanda excitedly said, "It is a *spool of thread*, exactly what Scott and Susan saw. All right, let's go!"

*   *   *

Looking straight up the side of the *spool of thread*, Amanda in awe, said, "This *spool of thread* is a lot bigger than it looked from where we first saw it. It's gigantic."

"Yeah, but do we go right or left?" asked Mathew.

Amanda, studying the left side of the gigantic red sandstone rock took a few steps in that direction before turning back to check out the right side. After a few moments of deliberation, she stated, "We go right. The left side is tight to the cliffs, there's no way we can squeeze through there. But the right side seems to open-up . . . just a little. So we go right."

Giving the rock formation a second look, Mathew added, "Good job Amanda. I agree."

A few minutes later, making their way around the *spool of thread* and into the mouth of a small canyon, Amanda beamed, "Wo-o-o-w, can you smell that?" Taking in a deep breath, she added, "It's not a strong smell, just a hint of the scent from all these flowers, like the smell of good perfume."

"Good perfume?" chuckled Mathew. "How do I know what good perfume smells like? The only perfume I've ever seen you 'dab on' is the rose water I got for you at the corner drug store."

Amanda raised her eyebrows, turned her head towards Mathew, and gave him a look that said, "Very funny. You're hilarious. Now, give it a rest."

Ignoring her *look*, Mathew breathed in all the smells of the small canyon and said, "But yeah, this smell is heavenly. And look at all the colors, so bright and vibrant. This is a great place to hide a clue."

"Okay, enough already. Let's find the petroglyphs." Taking hold of Mathew's arm, Amanda led Mathew further into the canyon. Scrutinizing the sides of the canyon, Amanda added, "Scott Montgomery said the petroglyphs were in plain sight about four feet above the ground under an overhang of red sandstone." Not seeing anything obvious, she stated, "Mathew you take the right side, and I'll take the left. It's a relatively small area so it shouldn't take long." Giving Mathew a quick kiss and a push to the right, Amanda headed off to the left.

Brushing aside a few branches from a cluster of chaparral,

Mathew made his way around a chunk of sandstone, the size of a small house that many years ago had broken off from the face of the cliff and fallen to the canyon floor. "Yo-o-o-o-o," shouted Mathew not more than two minutes after starting their search, "I think we've struck gold!" Looking around, Mathew saw no sign of Amanda. "**Yo-o-o-o-o-o-o!**" Mathew called out even louder, **"Amanda, where are you?!"**

Popping up from behind a cluster of gray scratchy brush, Amanda, wide eyed, yelled back, "You've found it so quick?!"

"I think so!"

Following Mathew's voice Amanda rushed over to where he was standing. Behind a small outcropping of red boulders under an overhang of red sandstone about four feet above the ground were the symbols:

Standing directly in front of the petroglyphs Amanda excitedly said, "That's them!" Using her index finger, she traced the outline of the symbols, "Here's the snake, here's the rat, and here's the shaman. Exactly as Scott Montgomery drew."

Placing his hand on Amanda's shoulder, Mathew, looked

down, pointed at the base of the cliff, and said, "And there's the butterfly just above ground level."

Following his nod, Amanda saw the carving of the small butterfly. "I can't believe it! We've solved the clue!" she shouted as she jumped into Mathew's arms.

Removing a small folding shovel from his backpack, Mathew began to dig. Not more than two feet below the surface, he uncovered a large brown glass jar at least twelve inches long. On the side in faded yellow letters and almost unreadable were the words *PEACH SLICES*. By hand, Mathew removed the last of the sand and carefully lifted the jar from the hole.

Looking up at Amanda, Mathew said with a big smile, "Are you ready?" Without waiting for a response he tightly grasped the rusted metal lid of the old jar and with a grunt twisted with all his might. The lid didn't budge. Taking an even tighter hold of the lid Mathew let out a deep groan, and again twisted for all he was worth. Again the lid held fast.

"I guess we can break the glass?" Mathew said looking at Amanda.

Pulling the jar from Mathew's hands, Amanda said, "It's not always about brute strength, it's in breaking the seal. Once the seal is broken the lid should come off easily."

Holding the jar with both hands, Amanda gently tapped the edge of the metal lid against the side of a large hard rock - rotating the jar so as to tap around the entire perimeter. Then holding the jar against her chest, Amanda gripped the lid and turned. With a little effort the lid unscrewed from the threads of the glass jar and flopped to the ground. Looking up at Mathew . . . she smiled.

Mathew smiled back and gave Amanda a pat on the back.

Looking inside the jar Amanda saw a dirt encrusted roll of oilcloth. Pulling the oilcloth from the jar, she brushed off some of the dirt and said, "Okay. Let's do this. I can't wait to see what happened to Scott and Susan."

Sitting on the ground, leaning back against the sandstone wall just below the petroglyphs in the shade of the overhanging cliff, Mathew and Amanda ate a few dried apricots and drank some water before Amanda began.

PART   THREE   (Scott and Susan)

Three Years After the Night of the Senior Prom: Age Twenty-One

"Scott, where do you come up with these ideas?" the instructor at *Cal Poly San Luis Obispo* said in an exasperated voice, his arms gesturing at the model of a house sitting on the table in the middle of the classroom. "How many times have we talked about this? There's no way anyone can build this!" With a heavy sigh the teacher continued, "Scott, you have a very good mind for design and if you applied it properly you could become a respected architect. But when I see something like this. . ." waving his hand towards the model, "I just. . . I don't . . . I don't know what to think. What exactly is it? It looks like a big rock." Looking directly at me and in a frustrated voice, the instructor continued, "How do you think you can build this?" Again waving his hand at the model.

I was upset and annoyed that the instructor didn't understand what I was doing. "First off," I said holding back my frustration, "the design was inspired by a *shell of a turtle.*"

"A shell of a turtle!" repeated the instructor as he closed his eyes and slowly shook his head.

Ignoring the instructor's comment I continued, "In Sedona, the desert turtle, to escape the intense heat of the day, burrows under the sand and at times all you see is the top half of its shell protruding from the sand. With a few modifications to the shell – doors, windows, and utilities – that's what you're looking at." After a silent pause, "If burying itself in the sand protects the turtles from the heat, I don't see why half burying a house in the sand won't also help keep the house cooler in the summer and warmer in the winter." Getting into the swing of my design, I was feeling better. "And the way you build it is much simpler and less expensive than regular wood construction. All you do is make a large pile of sand in the shape of a turtle's shell, which will take a half day at the most using a couple earthmovers. Wet it down and after a couple days the sand will have hardened into a giant sandcastle. Next you wrap the sandcastle in reinforcing steel and then pour the concrete. It would also be nice if the concrete was colored to match the color of the desert sand at sunset when the rays of the sun are turning the desert into beautiful hues of reds and pinks."

The instructor pressed his lips tight together. Still shaking his head, he said, "Beautiful hues of reds and pinks?"

I realized that the instructor was not going to understand my design no matter what I said, so to myself I thought, "Forget him. I know this will work." And so with nothing to prove, I smiled and with confidence in my design, I continued, "And lastly, using an earthmover, you drive under the concrete turtle shell and scoop out the sand, leaving a structure that blends into its surroundings, is easier to warm and to cool, and most of all the space will be fun and interesting to live in."

My instructor, trained in the classical style of architecture where everything was straight, flat, white, and typically balanced off with a row of fluted columns framing the entry, was used to reviewing my . . . unusual . . . designs. But for whatever reasons he never seemed to fully comprehend what I was trying to express. But this one, I called it my *'tortoise shell home,'* seemed to have really rubbed him the wrong way.

The instructor studying the model of my house asked, "There are no square corners, how will the furniture fit? And how do you put a flat door or a flat window in a curved surface?" With a quick exhale of breath, the instructor added in a tired voice, "Never mind don't answer. Turtle shells, sand castles, and colors of the setting sun are too much for me!"

Facing me, the instructor placed both hands on my shoulders and in a weary voice managed a tight smile before he said, "Scott, you can be a good architect. Just rein in your imagination and study the classics – the Parthenon in Athens, the Renaissance churches all over Italy, and in America study the proportion of the White House and the Library of Congress. You can learn a great deal from studying these masterpieces." With a final squeeze of my shoulder the instructor turned and walked across the classroom, out the door, and down the hall to his next class.

*   *   *

I hadn't seen or heard directly from Susan since the night of our senior prom where my last memory of her was the sad all-is-lost expression on her face staring out the window of the helicopter as she vanished into the darkness of the night.

For the first couple of weeks, after the helicopter had taken off for Los Angeles, I was more curious than concerned about where Susan was and why she hadn't phoned to let me know what was going on. In an effort to locate Susan and to find out about her mother, I contacted everyone I could think of who might have some information. I talked to the staff at the clinic in Sedona, I went to Phoenix and talked to the doctors, nurses, and orderlies at St. Francis Memorial, and I phoned All Saints Hospital in Los Angeles at least a dozen times talking to anyone remotely involved in treating Mrs. Cambell. Most of the people were nice enough and tried to be helpful but they just didn't have any information. The staff at All Saints said they knew of Mrs. Cambell and had treated her but couldn't divulge any medical information to me unless I was part of the immediate family. I begged for anything they could tell me about Mrs. Cambell and if they knew where her daughter had gone. Eventually I told them I was engaged to be married to Mrs. Cambell's daughter (a small white lie) and could they please tell me where Mrs. Cambell and Susan were. The staff sympathized but repeated that it was against hospital policy to divulge any patient medical information. Knowing that the information I so desperately wanted was known by the people on the other end of the phone, yet unavailable to me, left me dejected and feeling very frustrated. All I could do was leave my phone number and hope for the best.

Two days later, I received a call from one of the young female orderlies I had talked to at All Saints Hospital in Los Angeles. In a soft whisper, she asked me not to tell anyone about this phone call, as she proceeded to tell me that Mrs. Cambell had been brought to All Saints due to complications from a brain injury and from loss of blood - she had died shortly after arriving. The female orderly remembered seeing Susan and remembered that she looked tired and in shock, but was basically okay. She, however, had no idea where Susan went after leaving All Saints.

I was stunned that Mrs. Cambell had died. I knew the accident was serious, but I didn't realize it was . . . that serious. Instantly my thoughts went to Susan: she's lost both her parents. Her father a while back from cancer and now her mother from an auto accident. My mind raced. Does she have any other relatives? Where will she live? Where the heck is she?

I felt sad that Mrs. Cambell had passed, and I felt sad that Susan was going through this tough time without me. I knew she must be agonizing over her mother's death. But the overriding question that kept coming back to me over and over and over was, "Why hadn't Susan called? Why hadn't she written a letter letting me know where she was and if she was okay?"

I knew Susan didn't have any relatives in Sedona, so I figured she must have returned to Chicago for her mother's funeral. I knew Susan had lived in Chicago before coming to Sedona and that her mother had relatives somewhere, but whether they were in Chicago or elsewhere I had no idea.

Also, I had no idea what Mrs. Cambell's maiden name was. I spoke to a few of Mrs. Cambell's friends in Sedona to see if they could offer any help. I called a few strangers in Chicago who had the last name of Cambell, hoping they'd be related to Susan's father but I came up with nothing. I kept asking myself,

"Why hasn't Susan called?"

A few weeks turned into a few months and still no word from Susan. I was devastated and just couldn't figure out why she hadn't called. I felt horrible. I didn't eat much, losing thirty pounds. I avoided friends, not wanting to talk to them about Susan. Nights were especially bad; it was hard to sleep and typically I'd end up in that place between being asleep and being awake where my thoughts ran wild. Most of the time, Raymond James and I would get out of bed and go for long moonlit walks out into the desert and the red rock canyons. The nightly treks helped, but no matter what I did Susan was never far from the surface of my thoughts.

At first Raymond James was as sad and depressed as I was. He didn't eat much; he slept most of the day; and when someone came through the door, he enthusiastically lifted his head in hopes that it would be Susan and when it wasn't he'd drop his head and go back to sleep. Typically Raymond James would always come to work with me, but after Susan left there would be long stretches of time where Raymond James would be sleeping at home and I would be off working. He was no longer constantly by my side. He was no longer his high energy, curious, happy self.

But unlike me, Raymond James slowly made a recovery - he became more playful, he would jump into bed with me in the morning to get me up, he started to come to work with me again, and occasionally he would chase a rabbit or squirrel – one of his favorite things to do. Raymond James, however, was a lousy hunter; he never caught anything he chased or as Susan used to say, he was a great hunter - he just didn't want to kill another animal. Raymond James was slowly returning to all the things he used to do - he was returning to his old self.

Looking back at that time, I know this will sound crazy, but I truly believe that Raymond James broke out of his sadness, of missing Susan, because he wanted to show me the way out of my sadness – if he could do it, so could I.

One morning I woke up with Raymond James sitting next to me in bed. When I rolled over and opened my eyes, Raymond James gave me a little soft, "r-o-o-o-f." He gently took hold of my hand in his mouth, and pulled me out of bed, down the hall, and to the front door. As soon as I opened the front door, Raymond James jumped out. After a few steps he turned around and gave me a couple quick, "Woof, woof." Even in my depressed state, I wasn't completely out-of-it and could tell that Raymond James wanted me to follow him. Quickly getting dressed, I grabbed one, then two apples from a bowl and poured some dry dog food into a small paper bag and followed him out the door. The sun was not quite up, but there was enough reflected light from a full moon that we could see where we were going. Raymond James was in the lead with me a few steps behind.

Thirty minutes later we arrived at a small butte just outside of town, overlooking a large meadow to the east. Sitting on the edge of the cliff, my feet dangling over the side, Raymond James sat next to me. As the sun peaked over the distant hills I poured Raymond James' dry food out for him to eat and I took a bite of my apple. This was one of our - Susan's,

Raymond James' and my favorite places to watch the sun come up in the morning. We would often start the day by coming here before school.

That morning sitting on the butte, Raymond James had been very happy – jumping around barking with delight, chasing small flying bugs as they flew by, licking my face, and in general having a great time.

He came over, grabbed the sleeve of my shirt between his teeth and gave it a pull. "Come on let's jump around," He was saying. One last effort to break me out of my sadness. But I didn't move - I missed my Susan too much.

I didn't feel happy and I didn't feel like jumping around. I felt alone and sad and wondered where the heck my Susan was. This was *our spot* and this morning when I ran out of the house, I instinctively grabbed two apples, one for me and one for Susan. For an instant, I had forgotten that Susan was gone and now as I sat on *our butte*, feeling extremely sad, I knew that Susan wasn't going to eat this extra apple – she was gone and I didn't know if I would ever see her again.

Like I said before, looking back I can now see that Raymond James was trying to show me that I should be happy; that Susan would have wanted me to be happy. But, unfortunately, at that time, I wasn't smart enough to see what was going on.

"Raymond James . . . you are absolutely the greatest dog ever and you knew what was important in life far better than I did. I love you so-o-o-o very much Raymond James."

*   *   *

My dad could see my pain and tried to help by having man-to-man talks with me, but there wasn't much anyone could do. One morning, as I shuffled into work, Raymond James by my side - we were remodeling an old saddle shed, turning it into a small veterinary clinic – my dad gently put his hands on my shoulders, looked me straight in the eyes and in the most caring voice told me that he loved me dearly and that he understood the pain I was in. He said, "I've been there. When your mother died," he abruptly fell silent, blinked a few times, closed his eyes, turned away, and swallowed hard. A moment later he turned back to me and continued, "When I lost your mother, I thought my world was gone. Sitting in the waiting room of that hospital and then seeing the doctor as he turned the corner of the hallway and headed my way, I could instantly see it in his eyes. He didn't have to say a word. I knew my wife had passed. But then thirty minutes later when they put you, all of six hours old, in my arms. . . "

Squeezing my shoulders a little tighter, a slight smile spread across my father's face, and a faraway look covered his eyes. "At that moment, I knew I had a choice to make. I could wallow in my grief, bury my head in the sand and hope that the pain would go away. Or . . . I could continue to live my life the best I could . . . for me . . . for you . . . and for your mother and my wife."

In the same caring voice that my father had started out with he said, "You're walking around as if you're half dead, your clothes are hanging on your skeletal frame of a body, you can't focus and you're making too many mistakes on the job. You've become a safety hazard." With his hands still on my shoulders and his eyes still on my eyes, he said, "You have the same two choices I had. Are you going to wallow in grief . . . or . . . are you going to live your life?" He paused for a good thirty seconds before he opened the old wooden door of the shed and gently pushed me out. "Don't come back until you've made the right choice."

Raymond James scampered out the door after me.

My dad and my friends had good intentions. They tried to help, they tried to get me to be the old me, but what they didn't understand was that I had lost part of myself, actually lost part of my physical being. There was this connection between Susan and me that bound us together - emotionally, mentally, and physically - and now that connection had been severed. **How do you snap out of it, how do you move on when only half of you exists?**

Whenever I closed my eyes, I would instantly see Susan standing in front of me – happy and smiling without a care in the world. The way she leaned to the right with her head cocked to the left as if she was waiting for me to reach out and take her hand. Her reddish-brown hair parted in the middle, the long front strands swung back behind her ears. The small scar just below and to the left of her nose where she fell on her bike, returning home after we saw, *Old Yeller* at the local movie house. But most of all when I pictured her with my eyes closed, I could see her shining green eyes looking back at me. The same green eyes I first saw in the barn those many years ago at the age of eight.

And then . . . when I opened my eyes, she would be gone. And I felt so very, very lost. I felt this deep aching pain inside of me, this aching loneliness, this aching broken connection that I just didn't know how to fix. I so desperately wanted my other half back.

*   *   *

Nine months after the night of our senior prom, I was sitting alone in a diner on Main Street. I was in the last booth in the back, swing music humming on the radio, I was picking at my burger not really hungry, when I heard a female voice a couple of booths behind me say in a quiet confidential tone, "Did you hear? Susan Cambell got married."

"No way!" exclaimed her companion, sounding surprised.

"Yeah, she did. I heard it was to someone back east and he's much older than she is and he's supposed to be very rich."

"No way!" repeated the second voice.

I didn't turn around to see where the voices were coming from. I just sat there not thinking, not feeling, not being aware of anyone in the diner, or for that matter anyone in the world. I just sat there staring straight ahead at a poster on the wall not more than six feet in front of me - Buddy Holly jumping in the air, holding a large serrated chrome microphone close to his mouth and shouting to the world his latest hit song, *Loves Made a Fool of You.*

Sitting in the back of that diner, after what seemed like forever . . . it hit me – Susan was married, had moved on, and was not coming back to Sedona . . . not coming back to me. At first I couldn't believe that Susan had left me – how could she? A moment later I was angry at her, then sad for me, then frustrated as all get-out, and finally I was super pissed off. Pissed off at the whole stupid situation. I was ready to explode. I sat up and gripped the edge of the table, planted my feet firmly on the floor, pressed myself against the back of the vinyl booth, looked straight ahead at Buddy Holly shouting his song to the world, and on some instinctual level decided that's exactly what I was going to do. I arched my neck and raised my face to the ceiling as I let loose with the most primordial roar I have ever heard. It started off deep inside my chest as a low growl and gradually rose to an all-consuming bellow. "u-u-u-u-u-U-U-U-U-G-G-G-G-G." It must have lasted the good part of a full minute.

I have a vague memory of the staff and customers of the diner looking at me and a big fry cook coming over to ask if everything was okay, but it was all pretty much a complete blur - I was focused on my rage, nothing else. Again, I arched my neck back and released another "u-u-u-u-u-U-U-U-G-G-G-G." Maybe not quite as dramatic as the first, but still very satisfying. As the last of the air left my lungs, I completely relaxed, my head drifted forward and rested on my hands lying on the table – my food pushed aside. I was drained and felt like jello, but at the same time I was famished. Sitting up, I finished my burger and fries, and then ordered two pieces of apple pie, and another root beer. The staff wondered what else I was going to do.

Raymond James was off to my left, outside jumping up

on his hind legs, barking and pawing at the window glass with his front legs. He had heard my primitive cries and wanted to let me know that he was there to help, in case I needed him.

I was no longer angry, or sad, or frustrated at not knowing if Susan was alive or dead. I didn't understand how Susan went from our senior prom to being married, but at least I now knew that she was alive and, believe it or not, I was relieved that she had moved on with her life. Taking in a deep breath, I relaxed and on the exhale felt better than I had in a long time.

I smiled at Raymond James on the other side of the window, and he instantly fell silent, stopped pawing at the glass, and focused on me - his dark eyes stared at me, his ears pointed in my direction, his nose sniffed the air. It was as if he sensed or as if he knew something had changed within me. The next instant, Raymond James jumped in the air, turned half way around, and let loose with a loud, "Yelp!" And then he did it again. Raymond James was beyond happy because somehow he knew my sadness had lifted - it was time for me, for us, to move on with our lives.

*   *   *

A month later, I piled a few of my belongings into the bed of my truck, Raymond James jumped into the front seat beside me, and we headed to California. My plans were to enroll in college - California Polytechnic State University at San Luis Obispo - Cal Poly for short. The college was known for having a respected architectural design program.

Ten Years After the Night of the Senior Prom:
Age Twenty- Eight

"Jim, tamp that concrete into the corners of the formwork really good, we don't want any voids once we remove the forms!" I shouted over the noise of the pulsating concrete pump sitting just below the discharge of the rotating barrel of the concrete truck.

"No proble-e-e-m-o, Mr. Scott. I've got it handled!" replied Jim with a grin.

"Fernando, how're you doing with the concrete? Should I order another few yards from the plant or do we have enough to finish this wall?! " I asked as I turned to look at the remaining formwork waiting to be filled with concrete.

"No, I think we're good, Scott!" Fernando shouted back. "It'll be close but we should make it."

"Your call!" I hollered back. Surveying the freshly poured concrete, I smiled to myself and shouted so that everyone could hear me, "Good job guys! Everything is looking good and you're doing a first class job! Excellent work!"

"Scott!" I heard a voice shouting from behind me trying to be heard over the roar of the pump. Turning, I saw Mrs. Kelly waving at me with a smile on her face, but not wanting to get too close to the splattering concrete and bellowing dust. She was wearing a muted yellow, low cut sundress which looked good on her tall, thin frame. The dress fell to just below her knees and most of her back was exposed. I could smell her perfume from where I was standing twenty feet away. Most of the concrete crew had stopped work to gaze over at Mrs. Kelly.

Mrs. Kelly and her husband were the owners of the house we were building. Her husband had cleaned up in the real estate boom in Phoenix and they had decided to build a weekend cottage, bigger than most houses in the area, as a getaway from the noise and bustle of the city. Walking over to Mrs. Kelly, I returned the smile and said, "Mrs. Kelly, your house is turning out great." Pointing at the freshly poured concrete, "This concrete wall is going to support the flat boulder acting as your roof over the entry way." Turning back to Mrs. Kelly, I smiled and asked, "What'd you think?"

"Scott, how many times have I told you to call me Maureen or Mo? All my friends call me Mo." Mrs. Kelly leaned forward and gave me a small quick kiss on the cheek.

"Of course Mrs. Kelly or . . . I mean Mo . . . Mo it is." Looking back at the half-built house, "See how the house nestles into the surrounding boulders as if it's a bird's nest waiting for the mother bird to return? And see how the long front wall of the house curves up to mimic the curves of the adjacent boulders? The curved walls are close to matching the color and texture of the boulders but not quite because nothing is as perfect as Mother Nature."

Raising her hand above her eyes to block out the sun, she squinted through half closed eyes to study the front of the house. "Yes. Yes it's looking splendid. It looks more like a piece of art than a house."

"A piece of art you can live in," I responded.

Taking hold of Mrs. Kelly's elbow, I helped her up the

unfinished path winding between the large boulders surrounding the house. "Come on up, let me give you the grand tour."

Pointing up ahead, I said, "Notice, Mrs. Kel . . . ahh . . . Mo, how when we round this next bend in the walk you can look to the left and get a glimpse of the house. Just enough of a glimpse to pique your interest in wanting to see more.

"Oh yes. I can see it." responded Mrs. Kelly.

"And then as we walk a little further, see how the large boulders block the view of your house, but as you round the last boulder, VOILA! There it is . . . the main entry to the house opening up in front of your eyes. And notice the front door, it's made from black oak and stained to match the color and texture of the pinion pines." I reached out and touched the scratchy leaves and branches of a nearby pinion. "Because of the color and texture, the door makes a connection with the pinion pines, and pulls your eye, and you, towards it." Looking at Mrs. Kelly, I added, "Exactly what the entry door is supposed to do."

With a look of enthusiasm, I smiled at Mrs. Kelly. "The whole experience of coming to your house - from parking your car, the journey up the path, and even walking through your house is full of physical, if not subliminal clues that gently guide you to the right or to the left so that you receive the optimum experience of seeing your beautiful home. From the moment you leave your car to the moment you're sipping a cool drink enjoying the view from your living room, it's a journey of adventure, fun, and learning."

Mrs. Kelly, getting excited about her new house, "Scott, that's why we hired you. You're more than an architect, more than a builder . . . you're . . . you're . . . I don't know. It's like you're leaving part of yourself in this project."

I raised my eyebrows and shrugged, "I'm having fun, Mo. I can't think of anything else I'd rather do. Walking through or actually living in something that was only a simple idea in my head just a few months ago . . . is . . . magical."

Stepping forward, Mrs. Kelly, gave me a quick hug. "Your excitement definitely shows in your work." Glancing at her watch, "It's almost noon, how about I treat you to lunch?"

"It's almost noon?" I said, somewhat surprised. "I'm sorry Mrs. Kelly . . . Mo, but I've got an appointment back at *The School*, at noon. I had no idea it was so late. Thanks for the lunch offer but I have to run. Next time lunch is on me." Waving towards the interiors, "Check out the inside. Call me if there's anything you weren't expecting." Shaking Mrs. Kelly's hand, "Sorry, I've got to run," I said as I turned and quickly retreated down the path.

"Fernando, I've got to go! Any questions on the pour before I leave?!"

Waving, Fernando shouted, "No Scott we have it under control! We can handle it!"

"I never had any doubts!" I shouted back. "Stop by *The School* when you guys are finished! I've got some cold ones in the icebox!"

As I made my way over to the trunk, I turned to look for Raymond James, and hollered, "Raymond James, where are you boy?!" Seeing Raymond James lying under an old gnarled Juniper, "Come on boy, lets go."

Raymond James lifted his head and ever so slowly stretched his neck and front legs; and then tightened and relaxed the muscles of his body and hind legs; and finally his tail quivered, twitched, and fell still.

A few moment later, "Dang you, Raymond James!" shouted Fernando. "I know you know this is wet concrete. Do you have to walk through every slab I pour?"

Raymond James, heading over to meet me at the truck, had taken a short cut by trotting through Fernando's freshly poured concrete leaving a very nice set of paw prints.

Fernando shouted, "Well Scott, what do you think?! Should I leave them?!"

Over the years it seemed like every house we built ended up with Raymond James' paw prints somewhere in a concrete slab. We'd pour and finish a concrete slab, making sure to keep Raymond James away, and when we left for the day the slab would be smooth and free of prints. The next morning when we showed up to remove the forms, without failure there would be maybe a single paw print in the corner of the slab, or maybe three or four along an edge, or a trail of prints heading across the middle. I have no idea how Raymond James did it.

Raymond James' paw prints became somewhat of a symbol for the houses we built. People would be walking through one of our houses and they'd see a paw print and say, "I recognize those paw prints, this must be a house by Scott Montgomery.

From up above, leaning over the deck railing of the house, we heard Mo shout, "I love Raymond James. Don't you dare remove those prints!"

"You heard the boss, Fernando," I said, with a smile, as I waved up to Mo.

"Woof," replied Raymond James.

*   *   *

I left *Cal Poly San Luis Obispo* in my junior year. I was tired of my instructors not understanding me and trying to force-fit my round designs into their square concepts of what a building should look like. I returned to Sedona and started a small design/build company with my dad. I designed the projects and my dad and I would then build them together. We were a very hands-on type of company, involved in every step of the design and building processes from the first concept meeting with the client to handing them their keys as they moved into their finished house.

We were fortunate from the very beginning to have had more clients than we could handle - turning away one project for every two we accepted. We just didn't have the time or manpower to handle all the work. We figured it was better to do our very best on a few projects, rather than a mediocre job on a lot of projects.

By this time, my dad was getting on in years and wanted to share his lifetime of building knowledge with others. So a few years after starting our small design/build company, we - mostly my dad - decided to start a trade school for students who wanted to learn about construction and design. *The School* was based on the principles of **Learn** as much as you can, **Share** with others what you have learned, and **Enjoy** the process. *The School* had a very hands-on learning style, where my dad and I held classes in the mornings and went out into the field for practical experience in the afternoons.

We started, *The School*, in a small log cabin built into the base of an outcropping of red sandstone cliffs. It was a beautiful site and we figured if *The School* caught on, we could always expand.

Well, *The School* did catch on. We obtained a reputation for producing skilled craftsmen and designers who not only did fine work but treated the clients with respect and honesty. My dad made sure to sprinkle in large doses of his *learn-share-enjoy* philosophy into each lesson plan. In fact he made a small bronze plaque with the words, **LEARN – SHARE – ENJOY** and hung it above the main door of *The School.*

Seven years later, it seemed like a blink of an eye, we had almost fifty students coming from all over the state and over four thousand square feet of new classrooms and administrative space. I turned the original small log cabin into my living space. The students built most of the new spaces as part of their practical work experience. We hired a few of the graduating students to work with my dad and me in our design/build company. Fernando, in charge of pouring the concrete at Mr. and Mrs. Kelly's house, was a graduate from *The School.* Other graduates became teachers at *The School* and the rest seemed to have no trouble finding jobs.

We never did come up with a good name for it, so most people just called it, *The School.* My dad had more or less, at this point, stepped back from actually doing any construction work and devoted his full time to teaching.

Eighteen Years After the Night of the Senior Prom: Age Thirty-Six.

The School was out for the fall break, the students had gone home, and my dad was visiting friends in California. He'd never seen the ocean, living most of his adult life in Sedona. My dad was sixty-one years old and figured better late than never. He was staying with a childhood pal who moved with his family to the Big Sur area to open a hotel. He was looking forward to exploring the giant redwoods and discovering the wonders of the surf.

I was on my own for the next ten days and was looking forward to the quiet solitude of an empty school. It was early fall, the weather was still summer-like and the leaves of the oaks were just starting to change into their fall colors before drifting slowly to their final resting place on the red soil beneath its outstretched branches.

I was sitting behind my old desk in my study, a flat slab of walnut resting on a couple tree trunks, daydreaming as I watched through a patio window the breeze swirl the white sail-like seeds of the cottonwood in small circles before eventually ending up in the corners of the patio walls; Raymond James asleep at my feet.

I was feeling happy, relaxed, and very appreciative of all that I had. Half mesmerized by the outdoor scene, I almost missed the soft shuffling of feet behind me at the door to my study. Not wanting to pull myself away from the calming view of the falling cottonwood seeds, I reluctantly swiveled around in my chair to see who had entered, figuring it was the neighbor from down the road who stopped by from time to time to check out our latest design projects. He loved talking architecture.

But it wasn't our neighbor standing in the doorway; it was the most beautiful person I had ever known. Standing tall, her shoulders back, her head raised, her figure as slim and fit as ever, her hair still a very soft red but now cut short above her ears and close to the nape of her neck, maybe a few extra soft lines added to the corners of her eyes and to the ends of her mouth, but most of all, even after all those years, it was her eyes I couldn't look away from. Those radiant green eyes, so strong and gentle and loving, the same eyes I had looked into a thousand times over the years as we grew up together. At that moment, sitting at my desk, I was so very, very happy to see that my Susan . . . had returned.

Instantly all the years slipped away. I slowly stood up, pushed the chair away with the back of my knees, and without saying a word silently moved over to her, spread my arms wide and wrapped them around her. In return she wrapped her arms around me.

O-o-o-o-o-o-h-h-h, I had never felt so good. Body to body, head to head we silently stood wrapped in each other's embrace. There was no yesterday, there was no tomorrow, there was only Susan and me.

After what seemed an eternity, I stepped back with my

hands still resting on her shoulders. Holding her at arms' length, we each looked deep into the other's eyes.

Suddenly, Susan blinked, shook her head and quietly shrieked, "Oh Lord!" Her voice trembled as she said, "I should never have come. I've got to go!" She abruptly turned and sprinted towards the front door. "I should never have come," she repeated.

Startled and thinking that I'd never see her again, I quickly said, "Hold on! Wait a minute." Catching up to her, I placed a hand on the back of her shoulder and brought us both to a stop just outside the front door. "What'd you mean you have to go? You show up out of the blue, after disappearing for eighteen years, and then say you're going to leave? What's going on?"

"I shouldn't have come," repeated Susan. "The second I saw you, I knew it was a mistake. And then when we hugged." She paused and took in a breath and then in a soft voice continued, "I was in heaven. Your touch made me feel so very, very good . . . not just good . . . it felt right. It seems so right that we should be in each other's arms. And then it all came rushing back to me; all the years we spent together, how close we were, how we shared everything – our feelings, our thoughts, our joys, our sorrows." Swallowing, Susan added, "I'm still so very much in love with you."

"Is that so bad?" I said raising my head to look at her.

"Yes!" Susan exclaimed with a frown. "Scott, I'm married!"

I didn't respond. I already knew she was married.

Turning, I walked over to a wooden lounge chair on the outdoor patio adjacent to the entry. I nodded for her to join me. Slowly, probably wondering if it wasn't a mistake not to make a run for her car and leave, Susan made her way over to the chair next to me.

For a few moments, we sat in our chairs, looking at each other – noticing the things that had changed and the things that had not.

From behind Susan, I saw Raymond James shyly stick his head out the door of the study. He was focused on Susan – ears pointed, nose sniffing the air as if he knew her but wasn't quite sure how.

Susan noticed that I was looking past her, and turned to see what had caught my attention. "Is that you Raymond James?!" shouted Susan.

I saw a glow of pure happiness emanate from her face, as she clapped her hands together. "Raymond James what are you doing over there. You remember me, I'm Susan. Come here boy!"

Raymond James sprinted out of the study, across the entry, and jumped into her lap. Barking with delight and licking anything within licking distance.

"Raymond James, it is so good to see you. You haven't changed a bit." Susan rubbed the loose skin below his ears and buried her nose into his forehead. "Oh . . . Raymond James I've missed you so-o-o-o-o much."

Raymond James wiggled and squirmed with pleasure, rubbing the side of his head against every part of Susan he could reach. "Woof, woof, woof!" he barked, and then after some more wiggling and rubbing, "Woof, woof!"

Still rubbing, scratching, and whispering sweet nothings to Raymond James, Susan looked up at me and with a puzzled expression said, "It's been almost twenty years since I last saw Raymond James, which would make him what twenty-five, thirty years old?" She continued to look at me. "Do dogs live that long?"

Ever so softly, I said, "That's . . . not Raymond James."

Totally flabbergasted, but still rubbing and scratching Raymond James, Susan said, "What'd you mean this isn't Raymond James? Would a dog that has never met me before act like this? Look at him, he knows me, he loves me, you can't tell me that he doesn't remember me?" Susan quickly added, "This has got to be the same Raymond James that walked home with us from school; the same Raymond James that looked after me on our hikes." Burying her nose into Raymond James' fur and breathing in, "This guy even smells like *my old* Raymond James."

"I can't explain it," I said with a chuckle and a smile, "This Raymond James is acting as if you're his long lost friend and he can't get enough of you. It's absolutely astounding and I can't explain it, but . . . this is the first time *this* Raymond James has ever seen you."

Smiling Susan said, "I don't believe you. You have got to be kidding. This has got to be *my old* Raymond James! He looks exactly like my Raymond James - black body and head, white legs, stomach, chest, and nose. And look at those ears, we always said that Raymond James had 'special ears' - one up, one down, one black, one white. And here they are – his 'special ears'." Grabbing each side of Raymond James' head, Susan rubbed her forehead against Raymond James' forehead, "Of course you're my old Raymond James. Aren't you?" she whispered.

Raymond James, lifted his head and quietly barked, "Woof, woof."

Looking at me, Susan took a deep breath and on the exhale, said, with somewhat of an awkward smile, "Okay, if this isn't the Raymond James I grew up with . . . then who is this guy? And what happened to . . . *the original* . . . Raymond James."

Looking at Susan, in a solemn tone I said, "Raymond James, died a while back. He was fourteen years old, which is a long life for a dog of his breed."

Susan gave me a questioning look.

"Border Collie and Lab," I said. "As you know, he was a happy dog; he loved roaming the canyons around Sedona, he enjoyed following me around – doing whatever I was doing, he enjoyed interacting with the students at *The School* . . . I would say he had a good life. Towards the end he seemed tired most of the time and slept most of the day, in my study, in front of the fireplace. One morning he just didn't get up."

I flashed on a memory of the *original* Raymond James happily jumping in the air chasing flying insects. I paused a moment and glanced out at the darkening sky. Tuning back, I noticed that Susan and Raymond James were both caught up in the story and both were staring directly at me. I smiled and continued, "My father and I buried Raymond James behind *The*

School in the shade of an old Juniper. "

Susan turned her head towards Raymond James, still on her lap, gave him a long look and then shook her head a few times to the right and then back to the left, before she slowly said, "W-o-o-o-w. This is confusing. I'm not sure how I feel. In my head, I'm obviously sad knowing that my *old pal* Raymond James has died, but . . . ," running her fingers through the fur around Raymond James' ears, "on the other hand, seeing *this* Raymond James on my lap, makes me very, very happy."

Susan looked at me and I looked at her. A few seconds later, with a big grin across my face, I nodded at her and said, "I think you should be happy."

Susan said, "I am happy, being with Raymond James . . . and being with you." Her smile broadened and after a moment's pause, "How did *this*," Susan rubbed the underside of Raymond James' chin, "How did *this* Raymond James come into your life?"

Leaning back in my chair, my thoughts returned to the first time I met the *new* Raymond James. I began slowly, "About ten months after Raymond James had passed, I was coming home from a hike up Oak Creek Canyon. The sun had just set, the sky was turning a dark gray, and I could see a few thunder clouds off in the distance with their tops partially lit by the setting sun. I was walking pretty fast – trying to make it home before it got pitch black outside, when off to my right I heard this little funny bark. I almost walked right by it but turned around to see what had made that unusual noise. From behind a clump of bushes out walked a small animal. Because of the shadows, I couldn't tell what it was. But this small animal wasn't shy. It walked out from behind that bush and kept right on walking up to me and sat down on his hind legs directly in front of my feet. He then tilted his head back and looked up at me with the softest black eyes I had ever seen."

I looked at Susan, hesitated and then stammered, "I . . . I . . . I . . . thought I was dreaming, I couldn't believe it. There, not more than six inches in front of my toes - one ear up, one ear down, one black, one white sat Raymond James.

"While I was trying to process the fact that Raymond James was sitting in front of me, this little guy reached forward with his head, grabbed my shoestring between his teeth, and pulled it loose. Looking back up at me, he gave me a tiny, squeak of a bark. I couldn't help but smile, thinking, 'This little pip-squeak of a dog thinks he can pull my shoe laces and get away with it!'

"Looking back, I can see that Raymond James was just trying to show me . . . who the boss was.

"A few moments later I picked the tiny fellow up, tucked him under my arm and continued along the trail." Shrugging my shoulders at Susan I added, "And we've been together ever since."

Totally amazed, Susan shook her head, "Do you realize how astounding that is?" Still shaking her head, she smiled. "You finding another dog the exact same size, shape and color of the *original* Raymond James? How is that possible?"

"I didn't actually find him," I said. "He found me. And yes, I realize how amazing it is." Giving Raymond James a quick scratch along his back, I continued, "Remember when William gave me the *original* Raymond James, back when I was just a kid? William found Raymond James almost the exact same way this Raymond James found me. Raymond James walked up to William just before sunset out in the desert." After a short pause, "So it has happened before. And you know there are feral dogs running around the outskirts of Sedona. So-o-o-o-o," I said slowly, "Who knows, it is possible there are other dogs, other Raymond James' out there running around."

Giving me a funny look, Susan said, "I suppose it is possible . . . but to tell you the truth, it doesn't matter. I just know that Raymond James is here and he's the best dog ever."

Susan leaned back in her chair and rested her hand on Raymond James' head, who was now resting beside Susan on the cool stone floor.

The three of us quietly sat on the front porch, watching the trees gently sway in the breeze and listening to the calls of the evening birds as they came to life. Glancing to my left I noticed that Susan had closed her eyes and seemed very relaxed. My breath caught in my throat as I realized that Susan was back, beside me once again – for how long I didn't know.

Leaning forward I gave Raymond James a soft stroke and quietly said, "Susan." I paused a second as she opened her eyes and smiled. "Even though our relationship hasn't turned out the way I would have liked it, I still care for you and want only good things for you." I paused and then added while looking into her eyes, "Are you happy?"

Hesitating, she stammered, "Yeah I guess . . . I'm happy."

With a grin I said, "That didn't sound very convincing."

Pausing a moment, I added, "What makes you happy?"

With no hesitation Susan replied, "My children." She sat up straighter, and a smile came to her as she continued, "I have two wonderful children, twins – a boy and a girl. They are seventeen years old and both are entering college in the spring. Luke is very athletic, easy going, has many friends, and has aspirations to travel the world – he loves to explore. Debra is also a good athlete and is much more competitive than her brother, hates to lose, and loves to come out ahead, especially against her brother. She's very smart, much smarter than I ever was, and she's received a small scholarship covering books and tuition from Princeton." Stopping to think about her children, she added, "At times I wonder how these two beautiful, talented people could have possibly come from me."

Patting Susan on her knee, I smiled and said, "I know how."

Standing, I walked towards the kitchen, "I was going to make some coffee before you came, would you like some?"

"Coffee is good."

"Milk, no sugar?"

"You remembered."

Returning with the coffees, I placed one next to Susan and returned to my seat. After an awkward few moments of silence, Susan, while petting Raymond James' head said, "What about you? Are you married?"

"No," I simply stated, with no expression on my face.

Susan waited for me to continue and when she realized I wasn't going to, said, "What'd you mean, *no*? No girlfriends, no marriage, no nothing?"

"Oh sure, I've gone out with a lot of different girls, even dated a few more than once," I grinned.

"More than once? O-o-o-h-h that really sounds like a big commitment," she laughed.

"Well there were one or two who hung around for a while, but over time we just grew further and further apart until it just made sense to break it off." Pausing I added, "I don't push it anymore. If marriage happens, it happens - if not that's okay."

"What about your father? I always liked him, how's he doing?"

"Oh yeah. He's still going strong. He's the best teacher we have at *The School*, all the students love him. He's visiting friends in Big Sur right now. Stick around and you'll be able to see him in a few days. "

Ignoring the comment about sticking around, Susan turned her head to look around the courtyard, took a sip of coffee, and said, "What is *this* place? Do you live here?"

For the next hour I reviewed my life with Susan, telling her about attending and leaving Cal Poly, becoming an architect and contractor, the basics of my design philosophy, and how my dad and I started *The School*.

In time the conversation turned back to Susan. Giving it some deep thought, I said, "Susan, why did you . . . really come back? If it wasn't to see me, because, like you said, 'you're still married', so what was it?"

Susan looked off into the distant pinion pines surrounding the front of the buildings and watched as a titmouse jumped from limb to limb, pecking at the bark, trying to find small insects to eat. Gradually she found the words, "My marriage isn't in the best of shape." She paused. Her face saddened and her eyes moistened, "I'd better start from the beginning." She took a quick look at me, then a glance at Raymond James, and then turned back to the trees and said, "Remember the night of the senior prom and my mother getting into an auto accident?"

"How could I forget?" I said to myself and then to Susan, "Yes."

"It was the saddest moment of my life," she continued. "Much worse than when my father died. I was so young when he died and my father died gradually from cancer. I was prepared. My mother's death was sudden and she was right next to me in that helicopter as we flew to the hospital. I could see her dying right before my eyes. And all the tubes and the needles and the noise from the helicopter, I was in shock. It was like a dream and I was moving in slow motion.

"Arriving at the hospital in Los Angeles, being swept along with the group of nurses and doctors, being told to wait in one room, then another room, and never really understanding what was going on.

"The next thing I knew, my mother's sister, Aunt Margret was there and she was telling me that my mother had died and that I was going home with her to New York. I was in a fog as we boarded the plane. The first day in New York, my Aunt Margret settled me into the guest bedroom of her house and left me alone. 'To rest,' she said. The house was old and massive, and needed a lot of repair. She lived there by herself, her husband had died many years before, and now it was just her and a lot of servants, housekeepers, and maids. Lying on the bed in that big house, feeling all alone, it hit me – I was an orphan. My mother and my father were dead and I had no one."

I swallowed hard, disappointed that Susan hadn't realized that she wasn't alone, she had me.

"And then I lost it," continued Susan. "I become depressed. I wanted to stay in bed all day, I wouldn't eat, I wouldn't talk to anyone, I didn't leave the house, I was constantly crying, I was a mess and I felt so sad . . . about everything." Looking very unhappy, she said, "And I missed you so very much." Grabbing the napkin next to her coffee, she blew her nose and wiped away a few tears. "Throughout my depression I always wanted you to be there. You had always been there when I needed you in the past; you were my support in life. But when you never showed up . . . I guess I got angry at you too."

I stammered, "But . . . but . . . but I couldn't find you!"

Susan, looked off into the distance and whispered, "I know that now. But, back then my Aunt told me that she had contacted you, to let you know where I was. But I found out later she never had. She wanted to follow my mother's wishes and make sure I married into security and safety - in other words, *money*."

Susan dabbed at the tears running down her cheeks, "After a couple of months of feeling depressed and all alone, Aunt Margret couldn't take it anymore and sent me off on a '*little vacation*' as she called it."

Closing her eyes, she slowly shook her head and said, "My '*little vacation*' was in a sanitarium. I can hardly remember anything about the place – it's pretty much a complete blank. I was there for over three months. From the moment I walked in the front door, to the moment I left, all they did was give me pills. The pills made me feel good, but somewhere in the process my memory faded. What they were, I have no idea. I was too weak and confused to resist. Thinking back, I guess it wasn't all that bad. The place was a big old white colonial style house with big wide porches where the guests sat in rocking chairs all day, looking out at the green lawns. The nurses and doctors were okay I guess. It's just that I have a hard time remembering anything."

I put my hand on Susan's hand and squeezed. She took a deep breath and squeezed back.

"After I returned from my '*little vacation*', still in a weakened state, I was more or less forced to take two little pink pills every morning and afternoon. They seemed to make me v-e-e-e-r-r-y-y-y docile and compliant. If someone told me to turn right, I'd turn right; told me to eat, I'd eat; told me to sleep, I'd sleep. It was as if I couldn't think for myself. And to tell you the truth, in my mixed-up state of mind I was still mad at you for not rescuing me from that nightmare."

Susan removed her hand from mine, and wiped away the tears. "My Aunt was used to living in that big house by herself and I could tell she didn't really want to have me around. After all, she didn't have any choice in the matter, once my mother died - I was dumped in her lap. Before I knew what was happening, she introduced me to a wealthy gentleman and a couple months later I was married." With tears flowing, Susan reached over and threw her arms around me and I returned the hug.

"Scott, I'm so, so sorry. Can you ever forgive me? We were so close and we wanted to spend our lives together and then I go and get married. Can you ever forgive me?"

Holding Susan tight, thinking about what she had been through, my eyes began to water. I softly said, "Susan, there is nothing to forgive. It sounds as if you were drugged and didn't have much of a choice in the matter."

Susan cried hard into my chest and I cried along with her; Raymond James whimpered on the floor beside us. After a few minutes she mumbled, "Not exactly what we had planned after our senior year in high school."

I kissed the top of her head, "No . . . it's not," I said, as I wiped the tears from my eyes with the sleeve of my shirt.

I noticed that Susan was breathing somewhat fast and her face was turning a pale shade of white. "Are you okay?" I asked, concerned.

Taking in a deep breath and slowly exhaling, Susan said, "Yeah, I'm fine. I was feeling a little dizzy there, is all. When I get excited or . . . emotional, I sometimes get light headed. It's no big deal."

"What do you mean, *no big deal?*" After a few silent seconds, "Are you sure you're okay?"

Susan looked at me and with a grimace slowly said, "I . . .

have an . . . irregular heart beat." Seeing that I was ready to jump in with a few concerned comments, she quickly continued. "Apparently, I've had *arrhythmia*, an irregular heartbeat, my entire life, but as a kid I was so active I didn't notice any of the side effects such as light headedness or easily getting tired. I wasn't actually diagnosed until I gave birth to my children. The pediatrician noticed my condition and said it was nothing serious and there was a good chance I could go my entire life without having any major issues. And I haven't had any major issues, just a little light headedness at times. Like I said, no big deal."

Looking at Susan, making sure her color had returned to her face and that her breathing was back to normal, I said, "Well, let me at least get you a glass of water."

She followed me into the kitchen, Raymond James close behind, and then turned down a hall to the bathroom to wash her face. Back on the front patio, sitting in our wooden lounge chairs, the sun thirty minutes above the horizon and a warm dry breeze rustling the leaves of the oaks, Susan smiled and said, "It's so relaxing here."

I remained quiet, making sure she was all right and with a smile of my own nodded in agreement.

"Woof!" Raymond James agreed.

Smiling at Raymond James, Susan turned her green eyes towards me and said, "I can't stop now! If I don't finish, I may never get it out." Taking a breath, she continued, "Max, that's my husband, Max Nelson . . . and yes, my name is Susan Nelson. Max is an independent purchasing agent for the railroads, supplying the railroads with whatever they need – coal for the engines, food for the diner cars, cleaning crews, ticket spools to sell, you name it, he supplies it. And yes, my mother would have been pleased. Max is very wealthy." Pausing for a moment, Susan frowned. "Almost immediately after our marriage I became pregnant with Debra and Luke. When I became pregnant I stopped taking those little pink pills they were giving me, and I came out of my fog and realized how much I missed you. But there I was, married and pregnant, and I figured that you had probably moved on with your life so what could I do but stay where I was.

"A few months into my pregnancy, I discovered that Max was sleeping around – a girl in every port, as they say. He had told me they were business trips. When I confronted him, he confirmed that he was sleeping with other women and that he had been doing it long before we were married. He told me he was going to continue to sleep around and there wasn't much I could do about it.

"Maybe it was partially my fault. Most of the time I refused to go to bed with him and maybe that drove him away."

"Susan," I said in a soft slow voice, indicating that in no way was it her fault.

"I know, Max is a jerk," she continued. "But I thought I could . . . help him . . . or I guess I thought he would change. But he hasn't." Susan gave me a sad smile. "In any case, I devoted my life to raising my children. They literally saved me; having them to care for and to nurture, seeing them grow into such fine young people. Along the way, Max and I have grown further and further apart. We argue all the time, over everything. I'm glad when he goes on his business trips and I try to avoid him when he's at home. But he provides me with as much money as I want, a fine home to live in, and he adores his children." Taking in a breath and then on the exhale, "You asked why I came to Sedona? Well I needed a break. I needed to get away from my life and just relax. And I remembered how beautiful Sedona was and how comfortable I was living here. So I decided to come back for a visit and see if I could regain some of the good feelings I've seemed to have lost. I had no idea if you were still here, but deep inside I guess I hoped that you would be."

Susan continued, "And then, just now when I first saw you sitting at your desk and we hugged." She closed her eyes and a slight smile crossed her lips as she relived the memory. "I can't remember ever feeling so . . . at peace." A few moments later, she opened her eyes and turned to look at me. "And then . . . I felt scared. I knew I still loved you, and I knew I couldn't leave Max and my children so I had to get out of here."

"You still feel that you need to get out of here?"

Looking at me she said, "Absolutely, yes! All the old feelings are resurfacing and the longer I stay, the harder it's going to be for me to leave. I can't stay."

I took her hands in mine and gazed deeply into her eyes. "Susan, I knew from the first day I saw you - on your eighth birthday in your mother's old barn - that we were meant for each other, and I knew that I would never feel as close to anyone else as I felt towards you and as I still feel towards you right now."

A wetness formed around the edges of Susan's eyes and

tears again began to roll down her cheeks.

"Susan, I want you to be happy, really happy in life and I think you won't be happy until you and I are together. You deserve to be with someone who treats you with respect, with kindness, with gentleness, with deep affection, and who will be by your side no matter what. Someone who will love you with his entire being. Your children will be away at college, you'll be alone in a big house, you'll be with a husband you don't even like let alone love."

Still gazing into her green eyes, I reached over and wiped a tear from her cheek, "Bring your children and come live with me here in Sedona. You'll be much happier and you deserve to be happy."

Using the sleeve of her blouse, Susan wiped the tears from her eyes as she said with a forced laugh, "What is this, a marriage proposal?"

"In a weird sort of way, I guess it is. But before you say anything, follow me. I've been keeping something for you."

Walking into the house, into my study and over to the bookcase behind the desk, I bent down and opened a cabinet door in the far bottom corner. Pulling a small box out of the cabinet, I set it on the desk and opened the lid. Very gently I reached inside and slowly removed a dried corsage of suncups, prairie fire, and sage.

"The night of the prom I never got a chance to give these to you," I said, moving closer to Susan and reaching out to pin the corsage to the left side of her blouse.

She didn't move or say anything. She looked longingly at

the corsage pinned to her blouse. Slowly lifting her eyes to meet mine, she stepped forward and put her arms around my waist. I placed my arms around her shoulders, and, together as one, we slowly danced from side to side, our feet shuffling back and forth.

She whispered, her lips close to my ear, "It's been eighteen years." She swallowed and added, "And I finally get to dance with you at the prom. Remember you did promise me the first dance."

I smiled to myself and squeezed her a little tighter. After a few silent moments I heard her whisper, "And you've learned to dance."

"Just for you," I said in a soft voice.

As the sun set and the room darkened, we swayed back and forth, round and round, to the silent music of our past.

*   *   *

The next morning, leaning against the hood of my old Ford truck, Raymond James relaxing at my feet, I waited in the driveway of *The School* – waiting to see if Susan would return. Last night after our silent dance, we'd stood looking at each other for what seemed like a long time before I leaned in and kissed her very lightly on the lips. After another long period of silence, Susan turned and walked out to her car, mumbling that she was married and never should have come. I followed her out and asked if I was ever going to see her again. She just stared up at me from the front seat of her car, looking sad and confused and beautiful all at the same time. Eventually, I said,

"Come back tomorrow around nine in the morning. I'll make a picnic lunch and we can go for a hike; no strings, no pressure. You came to Sedona to relax, so let's relax." She didn't respond. She closed the door and disappeared down the drive.

I hoped she would show up the next morning but I convinced myself that I would understand if she didn't. Having children and a husband, having a life on the other side of the continent, it would be a big step to make such a change. And to tell you the truth, if Susan did decide to leave her husband and become my wife, I would feel somewhat bad about breaking up the family. But I knew that I would treat her much better than her husband did, and I just hoped that her children would grow to accept me, at least as a friend. If nothing else, talking with Susan last night answered a lot of questions I had about what happened the night of the prom and why she never called to let me know where she was. Our talk helped me find a little closure, and I hoped it also helped her.

*   *   *

"Do you remember this?" I asked as I pulled the sage bush away from the face of the red sandstone cliff.

"Oh, yeah," Susan laughed. "And if I remember correctly it's telling us the way to go is straight up."

Susan had decided to join me and Raymond James that morning for our hike. She arrived in good spirits, laughing and talking as if she was a teenager. Her attitude was contagious and we both acted like youngsters the entire day: joking, exploring, and having great fun. And off course Raymond James joined in - barking, running in circles, and looking for as many rubs and scratches as he could get.

We decided we should hike to our *special place*. I hadn't been back since our first visit, all those many years ago. We were anxious to see if it still possessed that same magical feeling. We also hadn't forgotten that we had lost our virginity there, but so far we both managed to avoid the subject.

With a lot less effort than it took on our original trip, Susan and I had reached the medicine wheel carved into the face of the sandstone cliff and per my dad's original instructions, the medicine wheel was telling us to climb up, straight up to the top of the small red sandstone cliff.

A few minutes later, a bit dustier, a few scratches on our arms, and out of breath we stood directly above the medicine wheel, on top of the small cliff. Looking around, trying to discover the remains of a path, I suddenly felt Susan's arms around my neck and her legs around my hips - instinctively I took hold of her legs. Susan squealed, "I believe last time we were here you carried me on your back through this brush." Slapping my chest, she cried out with a laugh, "Giddy up."

Same as last time, Raymond James somehow found his own alternate way up the cliff. Seeing Susan jump onto my back, he also wanted to join in, so he jumped up to see if he could somehow grab on. After several failed attempts, Susan finally said, "Sorry Raymond James, only room for one."

Raymond James barked and then jogged ahead of us, apparently deciding to take the lead.

Susan was as light as a feather on my back. Just like last

time, I felt energized. Something about this place renewed my strength and made me feel . . . I don't know . . . I guess . . . kind of invincible. We quickly made our way through the overgrown brush, a good foot and a half taller than I remembered; Raymond James a few feet in front. Upon reaching the gap in the cliffs, Susan relaxed. I let go of her legs, and she slid off my back.

"That was fun," she smiled.

Holding hands, we squeezed sideways through the slot opening and into the grotto.

The sandstone grotto looked as enchanted as it had eighteen years before. Standing just inside the opening, we took in the smooth, sculptured, multi-colored sandstone walls surrounding the grotto in a warm protecting embrace; the babbling ponds shimmered in the rays of the sun; the breathtaking views of the desert; the inviting grass islands scattered amongst the fine red sand floor; and, best of all, standing guard over us all, the grandfatherly cottonwood stretching its branches out in all directions.

"Wow," whispered Susan.

"Wow," I whispered back.

Raymond James gave us a small muffled, "woof," and left us behind as he entered the grotto on his own. I wasn't sure where he was going.

Standing just inside the slot opening, Susan slowly turned her head to survey the inside of the grotto. Upon reaching the cottonwood, she noticed that something was different. Bending forward, she squinted at the tree to see exactly what it was. "What's that on the cottonwood?" she asked in a curious tone. "It seems to be moving."

Looking hard at the cottonwood, I saw the same thing Susan saw. Even though it had lost most of its leaves, the trunk and branches were covered in an iridescent coat of oranges and blacks that seemed to shimmer in the breeze.

"I don't know what that is," I said perplexed.

Taking hold of Susan's hand we moved closer. About four feet from the trunk, I recognized what it was. Reaching out, I gently touched the back of my hand to the trunk of the tree. Instantly, ten or so monarch butterflies fluttered away from the trunk and landed on the backside of my hand; they seemed to have been attracted to the dampness of my perspiration. The entire cottonwood was covered from the base of its trunk to the farthest tips of its branches in monarch butterflies.

"What're all these butterflies doing here?" asked Susan, not believing what she was seeing. She stepped closer and placed her own hand next to the trunk and a few moments later her hand was also covered in monarchs.

"No idea," I whispered back, not wanting to disturb the butterflies. "I know monarch butterflies only have a life cycle of a few weeks, and I know they go through this lifecycle - caterpillars that turn into cocoons that turn into butterflies - several times a year here in Sedona. And I know that they migrate south to Mexico each fall but I've never seen so many in one place before." I slowly shook my head as I said, "This is amazing. Who knows if this happens every year or if it's a one-time phenomenon? I doubt anyone is here to see it."

Astonished by what we saw, for close to thirty minutes we stood in front of the cottonwood watching in amazement at the gentle swaying of the branches and the slow-motion wave of the butterfly wings. Gradually we moved away from the tree and explored the rest of the grotto.

We noticed that Raymond James was fast sleep, lying on all fours, with his head between his outstretched front legs facing the great cottonwood, not more than five feet from its base.

Susan, looking at Raymond James. "Isn't that the exact same spot the . . . *original* Raymond James fell asleep on, last time we were here?"

We both gazed down at Raymond James fast asleep, looking so contented and peaceful.

"I'd have to say that's pretty much the exact same spot. And do you remember the *original* Raymond James had also immediately fallen asleep, and looked so . . . peaceful?"

"I remember," said Susan. Still looking at Raymond James. "And you're sure *this* Raymond James has never been up here before?"

Shaking my head. "No. Never"

Slowly turning towards me, Susan shrugged and gave me a funny questioning look.

Taking a step towards Susan, I put my arm around her. "I've stopped trying to figure out how *this* Raymond James seems to have similar memories as the *first* Raymond James. There are just too many similarities and I haven't been able to come up with any good answers." After a pause, "So, I just . . .

I don't know . . . I just . . . I just figure it's . . . just the way it is . . . and that's fine with me."

Susan nodded. "Okay . . . 'that's just the way it is' . . . is also fine with me."

The grotto seemed to be exactly the same; no indication that any other human had been there since the last time we were there. We spread our blanket on a patch of grass that faced the cottonwood and munched on bologna and lettuce sandwiches. We watched the quivering wings of the butterflies as they clung to the surface of the tree, softly moving their wings back and forth. We were mesmerized by the slow motion dance that took place in front of our eyes.

Pulling out an orange from the knapsack, I sliced it in two and handed half to Susan. "I have three more in the sack. Let me know if you want more," I said.

While sucking the juice from the orange, I noticed one butterfly leave the tree and make its way over to us. Holding out the orange, the butterfly gently settled on the rim of the peel. A few more butterflies left the tree and flew over to join the first butterfly. After a couple of minutes, my orange and Susan's orange were covered in quivering, dancing butterflies.

Getting up, I set the remainder of the orange halves next to the cottonwood and returned to the blanket. Lying side by side, Susan and I looked up through the branches of the cottonwood covered in monarch butterflies, silhouetted by a clear pale blue sky. The swaying of the branches was hypnotic.

"Are you relaxed?" I asked.

"Very," replied Susan in a drowsy voice.

"Do you remember the first time we saw a monarch butterfly together?"

With no hesitation she replied, "Sure. It was at my mother's old barn. You were working with your father. It was my birthday and you gave me a present. The present was a puzzle to find the monarch. Or I guess I should say to find the cocoon of a monarch butterfly."

"You remembered," I said somewhat surprised.

"It was the first time I met you. The day I met the boy who would change my life forever. How could I ever forget?"

"Do you really mean that?" I asked softly.

"Of course. You did change my life."

I reached over and gently placed my hand on her hand. A moment later I said, "I feel the same way about you. You changed my life the moment I laid eyes on you."

Lying on our backs, our hands softly touching, we looked up at the cottonwood and the sky beyond. I suddenly had an urge to roll over, give her a passionate kiss and . . . well . . . see what developed. I had the feeling Susan was having the same urge. But I also felt that she was conflicted about still being married. Some minutes later with the tension of *what-to-do* still hanging heavily between us, I jumped up and said, "I've got an idea. Come on. Let's take off our clothes."

"What!" exclaimed Susan.

Laughing as I pulled my shirt over my head, "Trust me, this is going to be great." Seeing Susan's apprehension, "All right . . . leave your bra and panties on and I'll leave my underwear on. It has nothing to do with sex. Come on."

After removing the rest of my clothes, except for my underwear, I reached into our knapsack for a large paper cup, poured a little water into it from our water jug, and squeezed the juice from the remaining three oranges into the water. Walking over to Susan, dressed only in her undergarments, I said with a big grin, "This is going to be s-o-o-o-o-o-o much fun."

Susan looked skeptical.

"Okay. Stand with your legs apart and hold your arms straight out from your body . . . like this." I demonstrated the pose of *The Vitruvian Man*, a famous drawing by Leonardo da Vinci.

Susan, still wondering what the heck I had in mind, slowly and cautiously assumed the pose. By this time, several dozen butterflies were fluttering around the mouth of the cup. Walking up to Susan, I gently kissed her forehead. "Close your eyes and stand still. This m-a-a-a-a-y be a little cold."

I then very carefully and slowly poured the orange juice mixture over her. Starting at the tips of her fingers, I moved up her arms to her head, up the other arm, down her chest, stomach, back, and down each leg. Standing back, I whispered, "Remember don't move."

Licking her lips, Susan said, "This is sweet . . . and good but why'd you pour it on me?"

"Shhhhh. Have a little faith."

The butterflies that had been circling the cupful of watered-down orange juice immediately fluttered over to Susan and landed on her arms. A few seconds later several more butterflies left the tree and made their way over to her.

With her eyes still closed, Susan purred, "What's going on? This tickles."

Grinning to myself, I watched as still more butterflies left the cottonwood and landed on Susan. I quietly said, "You're being covered in butterflies."

Quickly opening her eyes, Susan saw several butterflies resting on her arms and many more coming her way. She closed her eyes. "This feels so wonderful," she said, proudly puffing out her chest, standing a little taller, and tilting her head back. Within a few minutes every inch of her body was covered with thousands of beautiful monarch butterflies.

Stepping back a few strides to get a better look, my mouth fell open as I stood in awe. I was looking at the woman I loved, standing perfectly still, covered with butterflies in the middle of a magical grotto beneath a majestic cottonwood which also happened to be covered in butterflies. And above it all, stood a benevolent pastel blue sky. The sandstone cliffs, the cottonwood, Susan, the air itself all appeared to be shimmering with the colors of the rainbow. I was hypnotized by what I saw and my eyes moistened. I didn't want the moment to end.

I'm not sure how long we stood there, but eventually I noticed the butterflies making their way back to the cottonwood. Susan opened her eyes, smiled wide, and full of exuberance, ran towards me with her arms spread wide. As we collided, her arms wrapped around me and mine around her, she squeezed tight as she said with excitement, "That was so wonderful. I could feel all their tiny soft legs crawling over my skin, almost like a gentle massage. And what made it so special was that it was happening to my **entire body** as if I was wearing a skintight suit of tiny ultra-soft legs. At that moment, nothing existed in this world except the sensation of butterfly legs on my skin."

Breathing hard, Susan tried to relax. A few moments later she murmured, "It was a moment I will cherish forever." With her arms still wrapped around my body, and her head resting on my chest, Susan unexpectedly pushed me away to arms' length and said, "Why didn't you join in? Why didn't you pour the orange water over yourself as well?"

Taking a moment to think about my response, I said, "My original idea was to pour the juice over both of us, but then when I saw you standing there covered in butterflies and you looked so . . ." searching for the word, "Beautifully transformed. I didn't want to miss seeing you go through that transformation. If I would have poured the juice on me, I wouldn't have been able to see you. So I chose to share in your experience rather than go through it myself."

Returning Susan's tender stare, I looked deep into her brilliant green eyes and softly said, "Even though I wasn't covered in butterflies, I was experiencing it right along with you. Your experience came from being *inside the butterfly suit*, my experience came from *watching you inside the butterfly* suit, and we both shared the magic. And you're right; it was a moment we'll cherish forever."

Gazing at Susan, she never looked more radiant. Leaning slowly forward, my mouth inches from her mouth, I paused. We looked deep into each other's eyes, we smelled each other's scents, we breathed each other's air, we felt each other's bodies, and we heard the same sounds of the grotto. One of my hands caressed her cheek as my other hand reached behind her. I felt the soft warm curve of her back and pulled her close, the heat of our bodies coming together. I tenderly pressed my lips to hers and she kissed me back. My kisses drifted to her cheeks, her eyelids, her nose. I heard a soft moan as we slowly bent to the ground, our bodies pressed together, rolling onto the blanket.

*   *   *

Our return hike to town was a reinforcement of the closeness we experienced in the grotto. We never lost contact with each other as we walked along the trail; holding hands, holding arms, wrapping our arms around each other. We didn't say much, words didn't seem necessary. We felt close - bathed in the memory of the grotto. We didn't want to burst our perfect bubble.

Raymond James seemed to have had his own experience. On the way back he was full of energy and super alert, but at the same time was quiet and subdued as he walked along in front of us.

When we reached *The School*, we sat on the front patio in the same wooden lounge chairs we had sat in the day before. We watched the sun drop below the horizon, the low thin clouds glowing from the rays of the setting sun. Mostly we sat in silence, comfortable in the calm of the approaching night.

I left Susan and Raymond James with the sunset as I

went into the house to brew some coffee and grab a couple of blankets - there was a hint of chill in the evening air. While pouring water into the coffee pot, I heard the door of Susan's car slam shut. I heard the engine come to life and then the sound of crunching gravel as the tires quickly faded away down the driveway. The sound of Raymond James barking and his paws digging into the soft dirt alongside the edge of the driveway trailed behind her car.

End Of Part Three

Mathew lay flat on his back on the red sand at the base of the sandstone cliffs, just below the petroglyphs. His hands were laced behind his head and his eyes were open, staring up at the brilliant blue sky through the branches of a small pinion pine. He had been focused on the sound of Amanda's voice as she slowly read aloud the latest episode of Scott Montgomery's and Susan Cambell's story. After a few moments of silence, Mathew swallowed and slowly rotated his head towards Amanda, sitting a few feet away on the sand, leaning back against the base of the cliff.

Amanda set the last sheet of the story on top of the stack of papers resting on her lap. She looked up and turned her eyes towards Mathew. Neither said a word, both casually gazed back at each other. Eventually Amanda softly said, "That's the end of this installment. The only sheet left is the next clue."

Turning his head away from Amanda and back to the shadows

of the pinion pine and to the blue sky, Mathew said, "S-o-o-o-o-o . . . can you believe it? Susan Cambell left again."

Stretching out on the red sand next to Mathew, Amanda looked up through the branches of the pinion pine and placed her hand on top of Mathew's hand and said, "Susan had children. She wouldn't leave them. Neither would I."

"The children were grown," countered Mathew. "They were going off to college. They wouldn't even have been home most of the time. And her husband sounded like a complete jerk. There's no reason to stay with someone who's always going on business trips and cheating on you."

"I'm not sure I agree," said Amanda, still touching Mathew's hand and staring up at the branches of the pine. "Family is important, regardless of whether it's a good marriage or a bad one. It's hard to pull away from something you've been attached to for half your life. And your children never really grow up. They'll always need their mother. Sometimes a person needs to make a sacrifice for the good of others."

Thinking about how Scott Montgomery described Susan Cambell in the story and thinking about Amanda, Mathew stated, "You and Susan Cambell are a lot alike."

"Maybe a little," replied Amanda.

Smiling, Mathew said, "Maybe a lot." After a few quiet moments, Mathew added, "I think Susan will eventually come back. Her children will grow up and move away and she'll be left with a ding-wad of a husband. She'll come to her senses, dump him, and return to Sedona and to Scott Montgomery."

Slowly shaking her head, Amanda replied almost in a whisper, "I don't think so."

Jumping up and brushing the sand from his backside, Mathew quickly said, "Okay, where's the next clue?" Bending over, he picked up the final piece of paper from the oilcloth.

Clue No. Three

Congratulations on making it this far. You're almost there, just one more clue. Are the suncups and prairie fires in bloom? Best smell in the world.

Mathew stopped reading and said, "Okay, here we go Amanda. The last clue. We're finally going to find out what happened between Scott and Susan."

Amanda, now standing next to Mathew, punched him in the arm, "Enough already, keep reading."

This could be your easiest clue yet . . . or it may just be your most difficult. Whether or not you make it to your final destination may not be up to you or up to my directions - it may depend on whether the spiritual forces of Sedona want you to find this place. But if the forces favor you . . . by revealing this place to you . . . you will be in for the treat of your life. You will be experiencing the most magical place on God's green earth – Susan's and my *Special Place*, the sandstone grotto.

Punching Mathew in the arm for a second time, Amanda enthusiastically said, "Mathew, we're going to the sandstone grotto. Can you believe it?" Pausing, Amanda added, "I feel so honored. This is going to be great." Punching Mathew for a third time, "Keep reading. Hurry up, let's see what the clue says."

The directions I'm giving you are the exact same directions my dad gave me those many years ago when Susan and I made our way for the first time to the sandstone grotto. It's a three-hour hike in and another three hours back. Bring food, plenty of water, and don't forget to have fun. Here are the directions:

Step One: Che-Ah-Chi
Step Two: Path of the Setting Sun
Step Three: Twin Ears of Corn
Step Four: Follow the Universal Symbol of Oneness
Step Five: Under the Butterfly – Under the Grandfather

"Here we go again!" sighed Amanda. "I have no idea what any of that means. What in the world is *Che–Ah–Chi*?"

"Gesundheit!" grinned Mathew.

A moment later, realizing that Mathew had made a joke, Amanda politely chuckled and with a smirk said, "Ha! Ha! Very funny. You can be such a goof ball at times."

Pleased with his joke and still grinning, Mathew said, "We'll figure it out," as he reached over and pulled Amanda into a bear hug. "We've solved all the other clues, no reason we can't get this one too."

Tucking her head against Mathew's chest, Amanda mumbled, "I hope we can use Google."

Three Days After Reading The Latest Clue - Clue Three

Mathew had spent most of the last three days trying to decipher the directions to the sandstone grotto left by Scott Montgomery in his latest clue. He searched, found, and met with several longtime residents of Sedona. He asked them questions, probed their memories, and hoped they could offer some sort of guidance as to how to unravel the mysteries of the clue. He searched the shelves of old book stores, had long conversations with hikers and naturalists, and he followed up on every lead he'd found. But what he hadn't done, was let anyone know exactly why he'd been asking all those questions. Mathew and Amanda respected Scott's and Susan's wish of keeping the sandstone grotto a secret and they were trying to do the same.

While Mathew searched for the answers to the clues, Amanda had been working on fixing up their Sedona house. First she cleaned everything . . . twice . . . spider webs, leaves, rodent's nests, and everything else you could imagine – remember the house was old and had sat vacant for the last ten years. She scraped the walls and ceiling of old paint, patched holes, and then primed and repainted everything. She replaced broken window glass, replaced missing or damaged wood flooring, and in general had done a great job. Every time Mathew jumped in to help with the repairs, Amanda pushed him away, saying, "The faster you solve the clue, the faster we can find out what happened to Scott and Susan. I've got the house covered. You handle the clue."

Five Days After Reading The Latest Clue - Clue Three

Looking around at all the cars and people, Amanda said, "You sure this is the right place? You sure this is where the clue is telling us to start from?"

Standing next to their car, parked at the trailhead, Mathew, a bit surprised and frustrated by all the people, gruffly said, "Wife . . . you always ask the same question and I always give the same response . . . no, I'm not one hundred percent sure this is the answer, but it's the best we have." Looking around, he added with a frown, "What's with all these people? I thought no one knew about this place."

Walking around the rear of the car, Amanda joined Mathew and said, "Maybe this isn't the right trailhead?"

"I asked the lady at the bookstore, and she told me that she's lived in Sedona for forty years and this is the only trailhead leading into *Che–Ah–Chi* . . . and she should know."

"Maybe we got **Step One** of the clue wrong? What does *Che–Ah–Chi* mean?"

Mathew, becoming irritated with all the people and with all the questions, said with a huff, "If there is one thing I got right about this clue, it's **Step One**. I found an old Apache translation in a book at the library and *Che–Ah–Chi* is Apache for *Red Rock Canyon* and then in parentheses it said, *Boynton Canyon*. We are definitely in the right place and this is the only trailhead leading up into Boynton Canyon."

Grumbling Mathew took hold of Amanda's elbow and hurried over to the beginning of the trail. "Let's move out. Maybe we can lose all these people on the trail."

Looking at the numerous trails leading off in all directions from the parking area, Amanda said, "Which trail? It's a maze."

"The clue says, *Path of the Setting Sun.* The sun sets in the west so I suspect we take the trail that's furthest to the west."

"Are you sure?" whispered Amanda.

Agitated from all her questions, Mathew quickly turned towards Amanda, but before he had a chance to respond, Amanda slugged him in the arm and smiled, "Lighten up dude. Remember Scott Montgomery also said in his clue, '*Don't forget to have fun.*'"

After a moment, Mathew smiled back, "Love you Amanda."

Thirty Minutes into the Hike

"I'm absolutely sure this is the wrong trail," said Mathew, looking at the housing complex of red plastered condominiums situated directly in the mouth of Boynton Canyon. "There's no way Scott and Susan walked through these condominiums. Somehow we need to make our way over to the west side of the canyon. Right now we're more or less on the east side and these condominiums are blocking our path."

Amanda said, "How long has it been since Scott and Susan hiked these trails?" After a moment she answered her own question, "A long time. I'm sure things have changed and these condominiums weren't here back then." Pausing Amanda continued, "Let's keep going. This trail will probably take us past the condominiums and then we can head off-trail to the west and see if we can find another trail at the base of the canyon cliffs."

"I agree. Let's go," grumbled Mathew, quickly moving down the trail.

Four Hours into the Hike

"We're lost," complained Amanda, tired and sweaty, as she looked around for a place to rest. Spotting a fallen log under an oak, she staggered over to the log, dropped her pack and sat down. Reaching for a bottle of water, she took a long sip. "The directions said it was a three-hour hike in and three hours out. We've already been hiking for over four hours. We haven't even found **Step Four** yet and there's still **Step Five** to go." Sighing, Amanda quietly muttered, "Maybe the *Sedona energy forces* don't want us to find the grotto. Maybe we aren't worthy?"

Sitting down next to Amanda, Mathew said, "We may have taken a wrong turn . . . or two, but like you said things have changed since Scott and Susan were last here. I'm sure we're heading in the right direction." Reaching for Amanda's water bottle, Mathew took a hurried gulp and handed the bottle back. "And we did find the *twin ears of corn* which was **Step Three**. So we've got to be close."

Forty minutes earlier, Amanda had spotted the tops of two red sandstone boulders; tall and thin and looking remarkably like two ears of corn standing on end – kernels and all. They spotted a faint outline of a trail between the two ears heading off to the west, which they'd been on ever since. Calling it a trail was somewhat of an exaggeration, it was more like a small opening between the brush that followed a game trail that had been appearing and disappearing through the grass as they marched doggedly on.

"Well, at least we've lost the crowd," sighed Amanda.

Standing up, Mathew said, "It's got to be here somewhere. **Step Four** says to *follow the Universal Symbol of Oneness* which we're figuring is the Medicine Wheel carved into the face of the sandstone cliffs mentioned in Scott's and Susan's story. And the trail we've been following from the two ears of corn dead ends right here at the base of these cliffs, so it's got to be here . . . somewhere. Why else would the trail end . . . here?"

"Are we really sure that the Medicine Wheel is the *Symbol of Oneness?*" Amanda questioned. Mathew smiled at her and Amanda quickly added, "Yeah, yeah, I know we aren't a hundred percent sure, but it's the best we have."

Mathew pulled a folded pile of papers from the side pocket of his backpack, shuffled through the papers until he found what he was looking for and read: *"The Medicine Wheel is a symbol that all things on earth are connected to the oneness of the Universe. A reminder that all plants, animals, and humans are one with mother earth and father sun."* Looking up, Mathew smiled at Amanda, *"the Universal Symbol of Oneness."*

"I'm impressed," said Amanda.

"I did my research," replied Mathew.

Stuffing the papers back into the pocket of the backpack, Mathew said, "Okay here's an idea." Surveying the thick brush in front of him, Mathew continued, "Amanda, you stay here and rest. I'll take a look around and see what I can find."

Wiping the sweat from his forehead with the sleeve of his shirt Mathew closed his eyes, lowered his head, and tried to squeeze between the thick brush extending two feet over his head. The dry branches tugged at his shirt and scratched his arms as he plowed forward.

Sitting in the shade of the oak, Amanda poured some water onto a handkerchief and used it to wipe her face and arms with. Leaning against the trunk of the old tree, she relaxed back into the oak and immediately had a feeling of being cradled by the smooth gnarled bark. She closed her eyes, let out a breath of air, and was instantly covered in a warm soothing blanket of relaxation. Just before nodding off to sleep, a very clear and distinct image of a half circle flashed across her eye lids. Instantly opening her eyes, Amanda wondered if she had really seen anything or if it was just a dream. Figuring it was nothing, she closed her eyes and settled back into the old oak. Again, almost before she had time to settle in, the same image flashed across her mind's eye – the image was of the upper portion of a small half circle with a line protruding up through the top of the circle. She could see the image just above the top of a wall of brush.

Quickly opening her eyes, the image of the half circle with the protruding line . . . **did not, as she was expecting, disappear. It was right there in front of her, carved into the face of the sandstone wall.** Not believing what she was seeing, she shook her head and blinked rapidly. The image remained solidly in front of her. Leaning forward and focusing on the half circle, Amanda tried to figure out if she was looking at something real or only an illusion. Squinting harder she realized that the image of the circle and the line were real and were directly in front of where she was sitting, not ten feet away, sticking up above a line of tall thick sage.

"What're you looking at?" asked Mathew coming up beside her and taking a long drink from his water bottle.

"That," exclaimed Amanda, pointing at the symbol on the face of the cliff.

"What?" asked Mathew, staring at the place where Amanda was pointing.

"Right there!" Amanda said, pointing again.

Staring harder, "I don't see a thing."

Thinking that Mathew was playing around with her, "You don't see the arc of a circle right there on the face of the cliff? Right above the sage?"

Looking closely at the sandstone wall just above the thick brush, "No. There's nothing there."

"Look," yelled Amanda. "Right there!"

Pushing the scratchy branches of the brush aside, Mathew slid sideways through the sage, trying to keep from being scratched and poked by the sharp branches. A moment later, "You've got to be kidding!" he shouted. "Here it is! The Medicine Wheel is right here! We've been scouring this whole area for the Medicine Wheel and it's been right in front of us the whole time!" Making his way back out of the brush, he faced Amanda and asked, "How'd you know it was there?"

"I told you I could see it right there above the tops of the sage." Amanda turned to face the wall and started to point at the image . . . but stopped. Scanning the wall to the right and then back to the left, "It was right there. Where'd it go?!" cried Amanda. Glancing at Mathew, "You must have moved the brush and now it's covered up."

"No way," Mathew quickly answered. "The sage extends a good two three feet above my head and above the Medicine Wheel. There's absolutely no way you could have seen the Medicine Wheel from here, especially since you were sitting down."

"I saw it!" argued Amanda. "I don't know what happened, but I saw it."

Sitting down next to Amanda, Mathew took another sip of water and patted her gently on the thigh. "I believe you . . . kind of. But in any case, the important thing is you found the Medicine Wheel!" Opening his backpack, Mathew pulled out a banana, peeled it, and handed half to Amanda. "I'm ready to take the next step," said Mathew with enthusiasm while chewing on his half of the banana. "I'm ready for the sandstone grotto. What about you? Come on, let's go."

"You know," Amanda said, munching on the banana and pausing a moment to think about what they were about to do. "We are about to enter Scott's and Susan's *Special Place;* the sandstone grotto where Scott and Susan lost their virginity, where Susan was covered in monarch butterflies, the place that Scott said is the most magical place on *'God's green earth.'*" Looking at Mathew, Amanda continued, "Now that we're here, I'm thinking maybe we shouldn't go in. It's their special place, not ours. I feel a little like we'd be trespassing on sacred ground."

Putting his arm around Amanda's shoulders. "I know what you mean. I kind of feel the same way." Pausing, Mathew added, "But, I think we're . . . also . . . supposed to be here. What are the odds of us finding this story in the first place in that old desk? And then us finding all the clues and figuring them out? And if Scott didn't want us here, why did he give us the directions? And how could you possibly have seen the Medicine Wheel through all that brush? Something or the spirit of someone or the energy of Sedona or whatever you want to call it has been helping us, has guided us to this spot." Smiling at Amanda, "And there's no way on *God's green earth* we aren't going to take this last step, so get off your duff and let's go."

Smiling back, "You're right. I guess the *Sedona energy* is on our side." Amanda stood up and brushed off her backside before adding, "Because even though I can't explain it, I'm sure I saw the edge of the Medicine Wheel above the brush line and now I can't. Something is definitely going on." Picking up her pack, she added, "Come on, let's go!"

Twenty Minutes After Finding The Medicine Wheel

Almost in shock from the beauty of the place, Amanda exhaled very slowly and said, "W–o–o–o–o–o–w," as she stood just inside the perimeter wall of the grotto, looking up at the sculptural forms of the sandstone and the shimmering leaves of the giant cottonwood in the afternoon sun. Amanda leaned over and wrapped her arms around Mathew for support.

"W–o–o–o–w," repeated Mathew, his eyes wide and his jaw open as he wrapped his arms around Amanda.

In stunned silence Mathew and Amanda stood perfectly still as they took in the beauty of what was unfolding before their eyes. "It's like being in a great cathedral," Amanda whispered, not wanting to disturb the holiness of the place.

Mathew in a low voice said, "I know exactly what you mean. You can actually feel . . . the spirit."

Visually taking in the splendor around them, Mathew lightly took hold of Amanda's hand and together they slowly made their way into the sandstone grotto, Scott's and Susan's *Special Place*.

"I can see why Scott and Susan felt so strongly about this place," Amanda said, turning in circles to take it all in. "Smell the air, so clean and fragrant. And look at this cottonwood. I've never seen anything like it, so big and strong, and . . . protective but also very comforting like it's been here since the beginning of time." In wonder, Amanda continued, "And look at the sun diamonds sparkling off the ponds, and the undulating shapes of the sandstone cliffs, and the sounds of the rustling cottonwood leaves and babbling waters." Taking in a deep breath, Amanda sighed with pleasure. "It's so peaceful, it's almost overwhelming."

Walking over to a flat rock set low to the ground just in front of the cottonwood, Amanda stood on the rock, looked back at the giant tree and took in the colored sandstone cliffs, the sparkling ponds, and all the amazing scents floating in the air. She felt good – so good that she threw out her arms, leaned her head back, closed her eyes, and said to all the seen and unseen inhabitants of the grotto, "I can almost understand . . . I can almost *feel* the connectedness I have with you and with all things." A peacefulness fell over her; a feeling of peace she had never felt before.

A few steps away, Mathew murmured, "It's magical."

*   *   *

Mathew and Amanda found the last of Scott's and Susan's story wrapped in a battered oilcloth cover, buried under a small flat stone at the base of the cottonwood – a small butterfly was carved into the stone. The last step of the clue was, *Step Five, Under the Butterfly – Under the Grandfather."*

P A R T   F O U R   (Scott and Susan)

A week after I heard the sound of Susan's tires retreat, away from me, down the driveway of *The School* into the darkness of the night, I received a letter:

My Dearest Scott,

You have no idea how difficult it was for me to drive away from you that night. I want you to know that you are my one true love. When I'm with you the rest of the world falls away and all that's left is me and you – feeling so protected, and alive, and loved. When you wrap your arms around me, with my head pressed against your chest and I hear the rhythm of your heart in my ear, I know this is where I belong. I could very easily spend the rest of my time listening to the pulse of your life.

But my decisions no longer affect only me, they affect the lives of my family. I have a life on the other side of the continent, a house, a dog, friends, and two amazing children. If I divorced Max, it would devastate my children.

Yes, I know Max has his issues, but he's also got his good side and he's always treated the children with love. I just couldn't destroy their lives. I hope you understand.

The last time I said I love you, you replied that you loved me more than all the stars in the universe. Well, I still love you ... twice that much.

You will always be in my heart,

Susan.

Yes, I understood, but I didn't agree. I looked at the envelope, there was no return address.

Twenty-Four Years After the Senior Prom and Six Years After Receiving Susan's Letter: Age forty-Two.

My father passed away last week at the age of sixty-seven. He was on a construction site, doing what he loved doing most - teaching students the art of building. The students said that my father was observing the installation of an ornate arched entryway carved from the trunk of a giant oak when he walked over to the shade of a boulder and sat down. The students thought he was just resting, but an hour later when they wandered over for a break, they discovered that he had passed. They all mentioned how peaceful he looked. It was as if my father knew it was his time, found a comfortable resting spot, closed his eyes, and left.

The night before my father passed, as was our custom, we had dinner together on the front porch of my little log cabin behind *The School*. Almost every night just before sunset, he would stop by, maybe a friend of two would join us, and we would eat while watching the sun slide slowly below the horizon. Most of the time we would discuss our latest construction project or some issue about *The School*. Other times we sat in silence mesmerized by the beauty of Mother Nature – the setting sun, the clouds, the sky, the mountain tops fading into the distance. But that night, the night before my father passed, it was just my father and me sitting in wicker rocking chairs eating dinner and watching the distant views. Raymond James slept on an old threadbare rug with his back against the warmth of an outdoor fire pit.

After dinner my father's opening line was, "I've had the most wonderful of days. I doubt my description of it will do it justice, but I'd like to give it a try." He went on for almost two hours relating in detail every aspect of his day.

My father described how he woke up that morning to the warmth of the sun bathing his face. Slowly rolling over and opening his eyes, he saw beams of sunshine streaming through the windows with microscopic pieces of dust slowing floating to the right and then slowly back to the left – as if the world had shifted into a beautiful slow-motion dance. Even the morning sounds of the birds, just outside his window, seemed to be slower and more precise than normal.

Stepping out of bed, my father noted that the pains he usually felt in his knees were gone. After stretching he noticed, in fact, that all his little aches and discomforts had seemed to vanish. "Son, I haven't felt so good in twenty years," he smiled at me.

My father only taught one class that morning at *The School*, "Nature vs. House Construction." It was a two-hour seminar where my father would usually stand in front of the class and lecture, trying to get the students to ask questions and to get involved. "Today," he told me, "The shoe was on the other foot. The students were the ones deciding on which way the class went – doing most of the talking, drawing diagrams on the chalk board, and asking questions; and not your standard questions but in-depth questions that made me think before trying to answer them." After a moment's pause he added, "I was the student learning from them." After another pause, "One of my best classes, ever."

On his way to lunch my father walked past the local church, daydreaming about how good he felt. As he rounded the corner, he heard his name being called. Joanne Larkey stepped out the side door of the church, shouting to my father that he had won the raffle. She said that even though he wasn't present the night before at the drawing, he was still eligible to win. She went on to say that his ticket, he had purchased for the volunteer fire department fund, had been pulled from the barrel by the fire marshal and that he was the winner of a $25 gift certificate to *Lew's Hardware*. "Well what do you know?" my father said to Joanne Larkey. "Never have won anything before." Placing the gift certificate into his back pocket, he gave Joanne Larkey a hug. "This is turning out to be one nice day," he told her.

My father was having lunch with Miss Clark. If you recall she worked at the post office and helped teach me how to dance for the senior prom. Lunch was at her house and she had volunteered to prepare her age old family's secret recipe of lasagna with extra cheese – my father's favorite meal.

After lunch, my father leaned back in his chair and mentioned to Miss Clark that he was having a good day – none of the usual aches and pains, how good the students were in class, winning the $25 gift certificate, and now having his favorite meal with excellent company.

Miss Clark, thinking about the situation, walked over to my father, took his hand and said, "Maybe I can help prolong this good day of yours," as she led him into the bedroom. My father didn't go into any detail, but he had a smile on his face when he closed his eyes and thought about his afternoon frolic.

After lunch and after *the bedroom*, my father and Miss Clark had plans to head on over to the high school and watch the baseball game. My father had played a little baseball in his youth and had always enjoyed watching the town's high school team. He had even donated some construction material and a lot of time to help build their field.

The team this year wasn't the best team the school had ever had, winning and losing about the same amount of games, but they had one player, this tall lanky sophomore, called Blast, who played third base. Everyone called him Blast because that was the sound you heard when his bat connected with the ball. People said he was good enough to make it into college ball and, who knows, maybe even into the professionals.

"It was the top of the ninth inning," my father said, "Sedona High was ahead by one, but the visiting team had men on second and third with no outs and the opposing team's best hitter was up to bat. A base hit would win the game for the visitors. On the first pitch, the batter, a giant of a kid with arms as big around as small trees, hit a screaming line drive down the third base line. I heard the crack of the bat on the ball and then a blur shot towards the left field foul line. I've never seen a ball hit so hard. But in the next instant Sedona's third baseman, Blast, jumped high into the air, extended his arm as far as it could go and then the sound of the ball smacking his mitt echoed throughout the stands. Before the crowd realized what had happened, Blast pivoted in midair, reached out with his right leg and touched third base for a force out. At the same time the opponent's base runner on second was running full speed thinking that the hit ball was going to be a sure double down the line. By the time he realized Sedona's third baseman had caught the ball, he was three quarters of the way to third. Blast took a few steps towards second and tagged out the runner. It was an unassisted triple play, the inning was over, and Sedona High had won the game.

"The play happened so fast," my father continued. "There were a few moments of stunned silence before the fans in the stands realized what had happened. Then, as one, they all stood and exploded with applause. I could go my whole life and never see another play as beautiful as that. The play was poetry in motion, equal to any ballerina move you could see on the stage. I was fortunate to be there."

At the completion of my father's narrative, sitting on my front porch staring off into the darkness, my father said, "And now I'm having dinner with my son . . . and with the best dog ever, Raymond James. It is definitely a great day," my father smiled at me.

We quietly sat in our wicker rocking chairs slowly swaying back and forth, the scent of jasmine in the air, watching the stars twinkle high above in a sea of black. After a few minutes, my father said, more to himself than to me, "It was like a gift. It was as if. . ." he hesitated and then added, "as if God had given me this wonderful day as a gift . . . and I'm so appreciative."

The next day my father passed away.

*   *   *

My father was buried in the early morning of a beautiful spring day, under an old gnarled Pinion Pine, in a small arroyo east of town between two cliffs of red sandstone, overlooking the Cathedral Rock formation. If you closed your eyes and allowed your senses to drift away with the breeze, you could smell the rebirth of spring flowers as they opened wide to receive the morning sun, hear the flutter of humming bird wings as they floated from flower to flower – taking nourishment while spreading nectar, and feel the coolness of the breeze on your back and the warmth of the sun on your chest. It was a good day to say goodbye to the man who had cared for me through babyhood, guided me though childhood, let me have the reins through my rambunctious teens, and finally showed me, through his actions, how to be a man. Not just a man, but how to be a decent caring person who treated all living things with respect and love.

I loved my father very much and saw aspects of him in most everything I did for the rest of my life.

Thirty-Two Years After the Senior Prom and Fourteen Years After Receiving Susan's Letter: Age Fifty.

"Isn't . . . it . . . glorious?" said Mark Wolfe in a slow, loud distinct voice, as he raised his arms high over his head, tilted his head back and produced a smile as big as the auditorium itself.   The audience of a few hundred people applauded enthusiastically, as Mr. Wolfe pointed to the walls and said, "Look at those glass walls. Or should I say what walls? It's as if they aren't there, as if we're sitting in the middle of the forest. And the Aspen trees just on the other side of the glass walls, it feels as if you can reach out and touch them." Waving his arms at the ceiling he continued, "And look at this ceiling, have you ever seen such craftsmanship, such texture, such beauty." Taking a breath, he slowed it down, smiled at the audience and said in a more relaxed manner, "But . . . But my absolute favorite part of this building is the natural light." Again, spreading his arms wide, "Look at this light. Have you ever seen such a soft soothing yellow tinted glow in your life? I could sit for hours doing nothing but look at this light. The architect told me it's from the sun's rays reflecting off the yellow leaves of the Aspen trees surrounding our building, and then being diffused through the glass walls to us. It doesn't occur all year long. This tinted yellow light only occurs in the autumn when the leaves of the Aspen have turned and when the angle of the early afternoon sun is just right. And boy-y-y-y-y is it beautiful." The audience continued to applaud and after a moment, Mark Wolfe said in a low unhurried voice, "It's almost a religious experience."

A few moments later, allowing the audience to settle in, Mark Wolfe returned to the podium, placed his hands on each side of the top, leaned into the microphone and said, "As you all know we are here today to celebrate the grand opening of the Apache Heritage Museum, here in Flagstaff, Arizona, and to give thanks to all who gave freely of their time and knowledge in an effort to make this dream of ours come true."

The audience clapped as Mark Wolfe took a sip of water from a glass on the podium shelf. "We would like to give a special thanks to all the donors, large and small, who gave so generously. Unfortunately, there is not enough time at this moment to thank all of you wonderful people individually, but I encourage everyone to take the time to visit the bronze obelisk in the lobby, which has the engraved names of all the donors on it. Again thank you all for your generosity."

Mark Wolfe scanned the front section of the audience looking for a specific individual. Spotting him a few chairs back from the front row, he walked across the stage, closer to where this gentleman was sitting, and with a broad smile said, "In an effort to create this wondrous Apache Heritage Museum, I have worked with this next individual and his team, first through the design phase and then through the construction stage, for over two years. In the beginning, my goal was not just to convey to the architect our desires of what we wanted this Museum to be, but to somehow get him to . . . FEEL our desires. To somehow get him to . . . UNDERSTAND what we, the People of the Apache, experienced through the generations of our ancestors. I tossed out such phrases as: we want the building to reflect the history of our People; we want the building to echo our way of life; we want the building to make a connection with the earth, while at the same time we want it to touch the sky."

Mark Wolfe, facing the audience gave them a whimsical smile, shrugged his shoulders, extended his arms to the side – palms facing up, and said, "Touching the sky while connecting to the earth? What the heck does that mean? I had no idea what I was saying. I just knew it sounded good. Looking back, I see it now sounded more like a riddle rather than a set of instructions. I'm lucky the architect didn't throw me out of his office." The crowd erupted into laughter.

With the audience still laughing, he slowly turned his head from left to right and then back to the left, taking in the room, as he raised his arms above his head, puffed out his chest, and said, "And yet." And then after a short pause, "And yet, I believe the architect has solved the riddle. Have you ever seen anything like it? Have you ever seen anything more . . . more magnificent?" He paused and then shouted, "What do you think?" The crowd showed their approval with an outburst of applause.

Mr. Wolfe again looked at the first few rows of seating and said, "With the greatest of appreciation, it is my pleasure to give a special thanks to the architect and his team for giving to the Apache Nation . . . and to the world, this special gift. Thank you Scott Montgomery.

*   *   *

Over the years architectural styles have come and gone: There were the Colonial Revivals with their dormers and columns. There were the Modernists with their steel, glass, and clean boxy shapes. There were the Post Modernists (opposed to the Modernists) with their curves, and angles, and free-forms. After World War II, Tract Houses - row after row of small inexpensive colonial or ranch or Spanish style houses, popped up overnight to fill the housing need for the returning service men. Yet through it all, none of these styles really interested me. I had grown up in the deserts and cliff tops of Sedona. I had experienced how plants and animals had lived naturally and evolved from their environment. And to me that's what architecture should be - the buildings should evolve naturally from their surroundings. Each site was different, each client was different, and each building was different.

As I got older, I was fifty years old at that time, I noticed that people were either interested in understanding my designs or they weren't interested. And if they weren't interested, then no matter how much I tried to explain why I placed a pink boulder in a particular location, or why I inserted three small windows in a brick wall as opposed to one large window in a plaster wall, or why a roof line sloped to match the incline of the surrounding hills, they just were not going to, for whatever reason, understand my buildings. Which was perfectly okay, we all have our likes and dislikes and I'm sure there were things about them I wasn't interested in. In any case, the older I got the less I tried to explain my designs. I figured if I was successful in my design goals, the person walking through the building would experience what I was trying to achieve whether they were conscious of it or not.

*   *   *

One day a few years ago, Mark Wolfe showed up at *The School* and said that he had seen a few of my buildings. He mentioned how taken he was by their unique organic appearance and asked if I had a few minutes to discuss a project he was working on.

Two years later I'm sitting a few chairs back from the front row, listening to Mark Wolfe in the auditorium of the Apache Heritage Museum.

I didn't usually attend the opening of any of the projects I was involved with. My greatest reward was watching the owners eyes light up as they walked through their new home or hearing a joyful, "w-o-o-o-w" as they rounded a corner to experience a room or a view. I also enjoyed walking through the finished building by myself, realizing that a year ago the building was just an idea floating around in my head and today I was walking through that idea. Even after all these years I still cherished every one of those final walk-throughs.

Typically a few members of our team who worked on the project, a student or teacher from *The School*, would represent us at an opening or award ceremony. It was great experience for the younger members and most seemed to enjoy being in the limelight. But Mark Wolfe had turned into a good friend and he could be very persistent, so there I was at the grand opening of the Apache Heritage Museum.

The Apache Heritage Museum was one of our best projects: The Client, Architect, and Design were all on the same page and over time came together as one. The building was like a bird perched on a stone base at the edge of a five hundred foot high outcropping of granite boulders overlooking a majestic gorge and then gradually transitioning into a glass tower raising up through a forest of mature Aspen.

But, to tell you the truth, I had a tough time focusing on the grand opening and on what Mark Wolfe was saying up there on the stage. For whatever reason my thoughts kept returning to my youth, to my time with Susan - our walks to school, our hikes through the canyons, our quiet times watching sunsets. Once or twice during Mark Wolfe's talk, I would close my eyes and Susan's face would fill the picture screen in my head. On one of those occasions, with Susan clearly occupying my thoughts, a student nudged me and asked if everything was all right - saying I looked so far away.

I'd always tried to take life as it came, never tried to force-fit anything that didn't want to easily slip into place. Susan knew I loved her and I figured if she wanted to be with me . . . well then she'd leave New York and be with me. If Susan didn't want to be with me, I wasn't going to *force fit* her into my life. But . . . maybe I was wrong. At that moment, sitting in the audience of the grand opening of the Apache Heritage museum, I missed Susan more than I'd missed anyone or anything in my entire life. And it occurred me that Susan and I were both getting older and there was no telling how much time either of us had left. I figured there was a good possibility we'd never see each other again and that just wasn't acceptable. The thought of never seeing Susan again . . . made me feel . . . ill.

I'd spent my entire life in Sedona and hadn't seen much of the world. I figured maybe it was time to spread my wings and do a little traveling. Maybe even make a stop off in New York City.

A Few Days Later In New York City – The Day Before Thanksgiving

It all started eleven years back when Susan and a small group of her friends figured they'd share some of their good fortune in life with the less fortunate. The first time they shared their *Day Before Thanksgiving Meal* with the homeless, they had no idea what they were doing, but figured why not set up a tent in Central Park and hand out free turkey sandwiches and pieces of hot apple pie to anyone that passed by. That first year they handed out one hundred and twenty turkey sandwiches. Over the years, Susan and her friends, with donations from a lot of nice people, have kept the tradition going and have expanded the *Day Before Thanksgiving Meal* into the basement of the local Methodist church and, with the help of hundreds of volunteers, now prepare and serve close to a thousand hot meals. People are usually lined up out the door and down the block.

There is a three-block area north of Central Park where Susan and her husband had lived and raised their children. In the parkway surrounding this three-block area, the developer, to distinguish his houses from the others, had planted Red Maples. Some eighty years later these Red Maples had grown into mature sixty-foot trees with branches that reached from one side of the street to the other. These Red Maples surrounding this three-block area, acted as a barrier, protecting the houses within from the harshness of the City.

The people living within this barrier of Red Maples were like a small village; the neighbors looked out for each other's houses, they greeted each other in passing, and they all seemed to take on Susan's and her friends' *Day Before Thanksgiving Meals* as a rallying point to join together and reinforce the unity of their community. Most of the donations and volunteers came from this village surrounded by the Red Maples.

Thanks to the many volunteers, the basement walls of the church were decorated with finger paintings and drawings from the local schools. Ribbons and banners hung from the ceiling; the folding tables were set up and covered with festive plastic table cloths sprinkled with brown and orange and yellow paper leaves; paper plates and plastic silverware lined each side; and pumpkins sat in the middle as center pieces. The back third of the basement acted as the kitchen with volunteers, dressed in red aprons, scurrying around trying to get the serve-your-self tables set up with all the pans, warming trays, and containers of food ready for the first customer that walked through the doors. Behind them, stacked against the far wall, was the food – boxes of stuffing, breads of all kinds, tins of cranberries and canned olives, an assortments of vegetables, tons of apple pies, and hundreds of pre-cooked turkeys.

This year was extra special for Susan because this year her entire family – husband, children, and grandchildren were all volunteering to help out. Typically, one or the other of her children would be at their in-laws or busy with their own families to have time to make it to the *Day Before Thanksgiving Meal.* Her husband Max hardly ever volunteered, or for that matter, hardly ever made it home for Thanksgiving – typically away on a business trip. Max had made a specific point to attend this year and had several times mentioned to Susan that he wanted to talk to her after the event. Susan had no idea what he had in mind, but figured maybe, just maybe Max, because he was getting on in years, twelve years older than she was, volunteered because he was finally realizing there was more to life than making money and thinking only of himself. Susan had her fingers crossed. In any case, she was looking forward to seeing the entire family.

Susan recognized many of the returning people showing up for the free meals. Some had been coming since the first year in the small tent in Central Park. Some she didn't see, but hoped they had gotten a job and a place to stay and were having Thanksgiving dinner with their own families. One couple she saw every year was no longer showing up for the free meal, but coming as volunteers. Gary and Ruthanne, eleven years ago, were homeless and hungry, and Ruthanne was sick with the flu. Gary had lost his job as a laborer at a warehouse, their small house they had worked so hard to keep was foreclosed on, and they were living from one homeless shelter to the next. It was the low point of their lives.

When Gary saw that small tent in Central Park and noticed that they were handing out food, he closed his eyes and thanked God. When he made it through the line to the tables, Gary asked Susan if he could have two sandwiches, one for himself and one for his wife, who was feeling bad and was resting on a park bench, trying to stay worm. Susan gave him four sandwiches and unbeknownst to Gary, slipped a $20 bill into one of the sandwich wrappings. Years later, Gary had told Susan that those four sandwiches and $20 kept him and his wife going for a week. And during that week . . . their lives changed. Gary got a job washing the display windows at a local deli. The job wasn't much, but every morning before the deli opened, while the owner was inside preparing the days food, Gary would show up and put everything he had into washing those windows as if he was polishing the Hope Diamond. The pay was minuscule, but it kept Gary and Ruthanne alive that winter.

It wasn't long before the owner of the deli noticed Gary's work ethic and over time Gary moved from cleaning not only the front windows, but to cleaning the entire deli – restrooms, kitchen, seating and service areas. Within the year, Gary and Ruthanne were cleaning two other shops on the block and eleven years later they had a janitorial service that cleaned half the businesses on the west side.

Through it all, Gary and Ruthanne hadn't forgotten the generosity of Susan under that small tent in Central Park when they needed it the most - those four sandwiches and that $20 bill. Every year Gary and Ruthanne and now their two daughters attend the *Day Before Thanksgiving Meal*, not to receive a free meal, but as generous donors giving of their services and time.

*   *   *

It was close to midnight, the meals had been served, the tables and chairs folded up and returned to the storage closets, the decorations removed, the trash taken out, and the floors cleaned. Susan was standing at the exit door, ready to shut off the lights and lock the doors, but first she surveyed the room to make sure the place was clean and everything returned to its proper place. She was exhausted, but feeling good – it had been a great day.

Susan was so happy that she had spent the day with her family, handing out meals to those who needed them. A few times during the day while Susan wandered the tables picking up trash or serving second helpings, she had looked around to see how her family was doing. Once she noticed her son helping an elderly lady walking with a cane find a seat. Another time she saw her eldest grandson getting down on his hands and knees to clean up some spilled food at the foot of a gentlemen dressed in old worn clothes smelling like he hadn't had a wash in several weeks. Another time she noticed her daughter sitting quietly talking to a homeless young girl with her arm around her trying to help in whatever way she could. Susan smiled to herself, feeling so fortunate that she had such giving, wonderful children and grandchildren. Yes . . . it had been a great day.

Ready to hit the light switch, Susan felt a tap on her shoulder, jumped and quickly turned around.

"Oh, sorry to startle you," said Max, her husband. "I just wanted to let you know what a terrific job you did with the meals." Putting his arm through hers, Max guided Susan across the room to a sofa and sat down.

"Everyone did a terrific job," said Susan. "I think it was the best event yet." Susan had forgotten that her husband had mentioned that he wanted to talk after the *Day Before Thanksgiving Meal* was over. She guessed this was it.

Sitting quietly on the sofa, neither said a word. Max turned to look at Susan and said, "Honey, I want a divorce."

Susan was stunned, in shock, not quite sure what to say. She thought to herself, "He wants a divorce? I'm the one who should be asking for a divorce."

Years ago, ever since Susan had learned of her husband's affairs and his refusal to stop, they had been growing further and further apart. They had stopped sleeping together years ago, having separate bedrooms. But, both of them had been relatively okay with the situation, living their separate lives - Susan raising their children, having plenty of friends, and trying to help others. Max, busy making money and having affairs.

Seeing the look of confusion on Susan's face, Max said, "Honey, the kids are grown, we don't sleep together any more, I'm gone six months out of the year, and when I am home we hardly talk or even see each other. It's time we divorced."

Susan still stunned, only heard the word, DIVORCED.

"You don't have to worry about money or leaving your friends. You can have the house and I'll pay whatever you want. And you know I love the kids. I'll still see them and they can spend time with me when they can. We're already living separate lives, just in the same house. I think we both deserve better."

Susan knew she didn't love Max like a wife should love a husband. And she knew that she was no longer, if ever, physically attracted to him. And she agreed they were already living separate lives. "What about the children? They'll be devastated." said Susan.

Lightly placing his hand on hers, Max said, "I think you're underestimating our kids. They're grown, with children of their own. They've seen how we interact. They know what's going on. They'll understand."

Without another word, Max gently lifted Susan's hand to his lips and softly placed a delicate kiss on the back side. He then slowly stood up and faced her as she sat on the sofa facing him. Staring down into her green eyes, he gave her a small shy smile, shrugged his shoulders, turned, and walked out.

And there it was. At close to midnight, on Thanksgiving Eve, after serving meals to over a thousand homeless people, after seeing firsthand how mature and grown up and wonderful her children were, sitting alone on a sofa in the basement of a Methodist church, Susan came to the realization that she was going to be divorced. She thought about what being divorced would actually mean and gradually over a period of several minutes a smile began to spread slowly across her face and her eyes opened wide with the awareness that she would be free. She would be free to do what she had wanted to do ever since that dreadful night when she left the high school senior prom in the back seat of a helicopter headed for the hospital in Los Angeles.

Two Weeks Later – In Sedona

I was lying in bed, half asleep and half awake, tossing and turning, not wanting to get up and not able to go back to sleep. I was excited about my upcoming travels and was running the itinerary over and over in my head. I turned onto my side for the umpteenth time when suddenly I thought I saw or maybe I felt that someone was at the foot of my bed. Opening my eyes, I glanced down and saw a hazy looking figure standing a few feet away. Calmly I sat up, not sure why I was so calm. Normally I'd be a bit more excited if someone had broken into my house in the middle of the night. I blinked a few times and focused on the figure – it was a teenage girl, dressed in a sweater and a wool skirt down to her calves. Realizing who it was, a feeling of joy spread through me and a smile sprung to my lips. The girl at the foot of my bed smiled back, slowly waved, and then softly faded into the darkness.

A few moments later I woke up with my head on my pillow and realized I must have dreamt about sitting up in bed, because I was now lying down. A cold shiver ran up my spine and the hairs on my arms stood on end. And then it hit me . . . and I knew. I absolutely knew that Susan, the person I loved most in life . . . had passed on. My beloved Susan was dead.

*   *   *

A week later I received a package in the mail along with this letter:

Dear Mr. Scott Montgomery,

My name is Samantha Nelson and I'm writing to inform you that my mother Susan Nelson, you may have known her by her maiden name, Susan Cambell, passed away a week ago this Monday, in the early morning hours of December 4th. I was with her the evening before and she appeared to be in good spirits and good health. In fact, ever since Thanksgiving, she appeared to be more excited about life and the future than ever before.

She passed in her sleep, quietly and painlessly, the doctors said. There was no obvious cause of death, but she did have a condition called arrhythmia where she could feel light headed and tired due to lack of blood flow from an irregular heartbeat. The doctors are not sure if this was a contributing factor to our mother's passing. We felt no need for an autopsy. In some ways, it wasn't important for us to know how she died, but more important to us was, how she lived.

She is survived by her husband of thirty-two years,

Max Nelson, and by her three children: Luke and Debra

(twins) age thirty-one and her youngest daughter,

Samantha age fourteen (that's me). You may think that I

am too young to be writing this letter, but I'm very mature

for my age and even if I do say so myself, I'm very smart. My

mother always said that I got my smarts from my father.

We held a memorial service two days after she

passed. Many family members attended (children,

grandchildren, and relatives) as well as friends, and

families and children of people she had helped over the

years in one way or another. Did you know that my mother

had established a charity for abused wives and their

children? She also handed out free meals to the homeless

over Thanksgiving. She donated a good portion of her time

as well as money to her charities. She was a very giving,

generous, kind woman who gave freely to anyone in need.

There were well over a hundred mourners at her memorial.

Her husband, my father, Max Nelson, gave a very moving eulogy.

I will miss my mother greatly.

Even though we held my mother's memorial in New York, my mother explicitly stated in her will (she could be very stubborn when she wanted) that she did not want to be, and these are her words, "entombed in some stuffy old crypt." Her instructions were for her cremated remains to be sent to you. I should let you know that my father and the immediate family were dead set against sending her remains to you. We have no idea who you are or what your relationship was with our mother. My brother and sister and I, however, felt it was important to comply with her wishes and have convinced the others to follow suit. My mother also directed that the attached note should accompany her remains. I took the liberty of reading the note and I have no idea what my mother is talking about. I hope you do.

If you do not remember my mother, or for whatever reason have no intention of complying with her wishes, or if this package ends up in the hands of someone other than Scott Montgomery, please be so kind as to return this package to me at the return address on the outside of the package.

And finally I have a request of my own – Mr. Montgomery, if you do follow through with my mother's wishes, could you please send me a short reply, confirming that you received the package and that my dear mother has been properly put to rest.

Sincerely,

Samantha Nelson, daughter of Susan Nelson (Cambell)

Taking a moment to digest the letter, I picked up the accompanying envelope, tore off the end, and slid out the card. On the card, in Susan's precise upright handwriting, all in capital letters were the words:

BURY ME WITH THE BUTTERFLIES

*   *   *

I followed through with Susan's wishes. The day after receiving Susan's remains, Raymond James and I hiked up to the sandstone grotto – *our special place* - and performed a small ceremony committing Susan's ashes to their final resting place.

Along with Susan's ashes, I brought along two small pinion pines. I found a spot where I thought the pines would do well - plenty of sunlight, water, protection from the wind - and with my knife dug two holes about eighteen inches apart. With as much reverence and respect as I could muster, I planted the two pines.

I sprinkled Susan's ashes on the small tree closest to the pond and added plenty of water to each. My hope was that the water would soak down into the earth, into the roots of the pines, taking with it the nourishment of the ashes.

I sat there facing the two trees - Raymond James by my side, my eyes closed, my legs folded under me, remembering the person I loved most in this life; the day we first met on her birthday and discovered the monarch cocoon in the milkweed bush, the first day of school where I couldn't leave her side and later she kissed me for the first time. I remembered all the times we studied together outdoors under the oaks, all the movies we saw holding hands in the dark, our annual visits to the town carnival - riding and eating everything in sight until we couldn't take it anymore. I remembered walking home together after school, her arms wrapped around my arm, her head resting on my shoulder. I remembered Susan always turning the wrong way when we exited a building - I could never figure that one out. I remembered the smoothness of her hands; every look on her face; the feel of her hair sliding through my fingers; the warm, clean, fresh smell of her skin. But most of all, I remembered her radiant green eyes - the way they sparkled when she was happy or turned a shade of gray when she was sad or, when we were making love in this very same sandstone grotto, the way her eyes turned into the most loving, gentle, magical color of green I had ever seen. I had discovered myself in those eyes.

I didn't feel sad. I didn't shed any tears. I was past the tears and the sadness. I felt . . . I don't know . . . I guess you could say at that moment, I just felt so . . . very, very close to my Susan.

Four Weeks Later

One month after placing Susan to rest in the sandstone grotto, I sat by the fireplace in my office at *The School* - the weather had turned cold and a blanket covered my legs. Raymond James curled up on the stone hearth had his back to the flames. I still lived in the same small log cabin, in back of

The School, the same cabin my dad and I built and started *The School* in those many years ago. How time has flown by. I still taught the occasional class, but I was more of a figurehead rather than a teacher. A few former students were doing an excellent job of running the day-to-day activities of *The School*.

Sitting in front of the fireplace, I felt all the little aches and pains that came with age. I was still young, or least somewhat young in my early fifties, and my mind was still sharp or at least I liked to think it was, but my . . . *life force* I guess you could call it, seemed to have diminished. I seemed to have lost my drive for the excitement of jumping into my next new adventure. I no longer looked forward to doing all the little things I used to love doing – hiking the red rocks, fine tuning the design of our latest project, discussing the pros and cons of almost anything with the students, or the sounds of the many birds chirping as I lay in bed preparing to meet another day.

Ever since Susan appeared in the early morning hours at the foot of my bed, smiled and waved goodbye, my life has felt different, a little less bright . . . as if a light had gone out.

*   *   *

Hello, my name is William:

I am a Native Indian belonging to the Mohave Apache People living in the red rock area of Arizona. My father, also named William, used to work with Scott and his father, Mr. Montgomery, many years ago before *The School* existed. Scott was several years older than I was, but over the years he became like an older brother to me. When Mr. Montgomery and Scott opened *The School*, they let me attend even though I couldn't afford the tuition. And now, I suppose, you could say I'm in charge of running the school . . . now that Scott has passed away. Yes, I'm sorry to say that my brother has passed to the other side. Everyone at *The School* and in town have mourned his passing. He was a happy, giving person who loved and respected all of Mother Nature's creations.

Two days ago, I arrived at *The School* as I usually do, early in the morning before anyone else and entered Scott's study where I discovered his body slumped over his desk. I immediately knew that he had passed to the other side, that his spirit had left his physical body.

Raymond James stood at full attention and barked loudly when I entered the room. At first Raymond James wouldn't let me near the body, he was growling and letting me know that this was his territory – stay back. I gently sat down a few feet in front of Raymond James and waited for him to settle down – I knew that Raymond James meant me no harm, he was just protecting the body of his friend . . . his family.

After a few moments, Raymond James circled the desk, curled up into a ball, placed his head on his front legs, and looked up at me. I scratched Raymond James between his ears and told him that I knew how he felt.

As I approached Scott's body, I noticed that a desk drawer was open and in the drawer was a large envelope with my name on it. Inside the envelope was a set of instructions for me to follow in case of his death.

Scott had instructed me to sprinkle his ashes in a very specific place - a place very sacred to the Native Indians of Sedona. I was surprised that Scott knew about this place, but not that surprised knowing how Scott enjoyed exploring the red sandstone canyons and how in touch with nature he was. The more I thought about it, the more I thought that it would be the perfect spot for his ashes.

In his instructions, Scott explained that he had planted two small pinion pines in this sacred place only a few weeks earlier. His wish was that his ashes be sprinkled at the base of one of these pines – the one furthest from the pond.

In addition to leaving the set of instructions for me, Scott had also left the final chapter of his story. Yes, I have had the privilege of reading Scott's life story, the same story you have been reading. He told me that I was the only person other than himself who knew of his writings.

I was too young to have known Susan. She had left Sedona by the time Scott and I became close friends. For all the years I'd known Scott, he had never mentioned anything about Susan to me. But for those who knew him well, we could see that there was something missing in his life, and now I know . . . it was Susan.

I will tell you that my People believe, that when we pass over to the other side, our spirits take with them all that we have experienced in this life. And then, at some time in the future, our spirits return. In that new life we carry with us the events from our past lives. So even though Scott and Susan were not together in this life, I truly believe that in the next life or the next life after that their love will bring them together and they will be reunited.

Scott's final wishes were that I wrap my letter along with the last chapter of his story in an oilcloth and bury it at the base of the cottonwood. He also asked that I place a small stone with a carving of a butterfly directly over the spot where the oilcloth was buried. He had left the stone in the drawer with his other documents.

I have followed through with Scott's wishes in every detail. It was the least I could do for my friend and brother.

Raymond James came with me to the grotto to say his good-byes to Scott and afterwards I brought him home with me, where he lived with my family for several weeks. One day he disappeared. I don't know what happened to him, whether he had an accident, is living with someone else, or is roaming the desert. Occasionally, someone will mention that they saw a black and white dog with funny looking ears wandering around town, but whether that was Raymond James . . . who knows?

William Red Eagle
The School

End of Part Four

Leaning back against the old cottonwood, Mathew and Amanda sat in silence, staring off into the distant views. A black raven cawed loudly as it glided overhead and drifted down the valley. Several minutes passed before Mathew slowly shuffled the papers together, folded them in half, and placed them on the ground next to him, setting the butterfly stone on top.

Amanda, using the sleeve of her shirt, wiped the tears from her eyes, and then interlocked her fingers around Mathew's arm and leaned her head against his shoulder. In a soft voice, "I'm so sad that Scott and Susan never made it back together – not even at the end."

Mathew softly kissed Amanda on the top of her head, "Yeah, it is a little sad but like Scott said, he lived a full life doing what he enjoyed and so did Susan with her children and grandchildren and friends." After a pause, "And who knows, like William Red Eagle said, maybe the next time around they really will be together."

"Like reincarnation?" asked Amanda quietly.

"Yeah, I guess."

"I'm not sure I believe in reincarnation," Amanda softly replied.

"Me neither," said Mathew with a slow exhale. "But who knows?"

After a moment of stillness, Amanda said, "I'm also sad because the story has ended. Scott and Susan have become part of our lives, as if they were family . . . or best friends."

Squeezing Amanda's hand, Mathew slowly said, "I know what you mean. I was right there with Scott when he was showing Susan that monarch cocoon, and I could feel his pain when Susan flew off in the helicopter. It was all so real."

Cuddling in closer, Amanda whispered, "And I was there the first time Susan kissed Scott. I could see the surprised look on Scott's face when she stepped forward and kissed him on the lips." Amanda smiled at the memory. "I feel so close to Susan, it was as if I was kissing you . . . or I mean Scott . . . or I don't know what I mean. At times we all seemed to blend together – me and you and Scott and Susan."

Ten minutes passed in silence. Feeling warmed by the sun, Mathew gently said, "I don't want to leave. I'm so comfortable holding you close and leaning back against this old grandfather of a cottonwood."

"I don't want to leave either," responded Amanda.

Several minutes later, Amanda gently sat up. Taking hold of Mathew's hands she gave him a pull, "Let's see if we can find the two pinion pines that Scott planted."

Hand in hand, Mathew and Amanda slowly turned in place as they scanned the grotto looking for the pines.

"I don't see any pinions," said Amanda.

"Hold on," added Mathew. "They have to be here somewhere."

Noticing an irregular shaped shadow on the face of the sandstone wall, Mathew pointing to the shadow, said, "Let's look over there. It looks like there could be an opening."

Hand in hand, Mathew led Amanda around the cottonwood to the far side of the grotto. Rounding a curve in the smooth sandstone walls, towering fifty feet over their heads, they discovered a round alcove about twenty feet across – a smaller version of the larger grotto. But instead of a giant cottonwood - two medium-sized pinion pines stood directly in the center of the alcove.

Seeing the two pines, Mathew and Amanda abruptly stopped; Mathew's back stiffened, his eyes narrowed and his lips squeezed tight.

"I . . . I . . . don . . . don't believe it!" stammered Mathew.

"It's impossible!" exclaimed Amanda.

"How can this possibly be?" Mathew said.

Fifteen feet in front of them stood the sculpture of *Togetherness*. Or at least a rougher smaller version of Mathew's sculpture that sat in the atrium of the *TOGETHERNESS* Restaurant.

Stunned by what he saw, Mathew choked out, "How could these trees match my sculpture?" Thinking about what he had just said, Mathew corrected himself, "Or I mean, since these trees have been here longer than my sculpture, how could my sculpture possibly match these trees? I've never seen these trees before!"

The two pinions, sitting in the center of the alcove, almost five feet tall, seemed to have merged into each other, into one tree – similar to the *togetherness* sculpture. The trunks of each tree originally planted eighteen inches apart had grown towards each other. About twelve inches above the ground, the two trunks had merged, their branches twisting and turning and intermingling into what could only be described as a loving embrace. At first Mathew had trouble distinguishing where one tree started and where the other ended. But on closer inspection, he saw the outline of the two trees – the first tree gently merged into the second as the second accepted the first, and then the second gradually merged forward and back onto the first. It was the perfect balance of giving and taking. The pinion closest to the pond was a little smoother and more feminine than the rougher, larger pinion furthest from the pond.

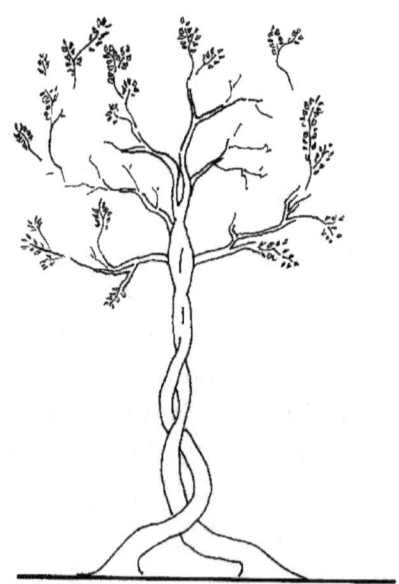

Stepping closer, Amanda studied the two pines. "They do look similar to your sculpture." Shaking her head, "But it can't be. It's just a coincidence."

"No," Mathew firmly stated. Stepping closer to the two pines. "It isn't a coincidence. My sculpture and these pines are almost identical – too many of the details are just too close. And I should know, I designed the thing."

Bewildered, Mathew and Amanda walked around the pinions that had started off as two and then over time had become one.

Sitting in the shade of the sandstone cliffs, Mathew and Amanda stared at the two trees. Neither said a word as they both contemplated how Mathew's sculpture could have possibly ended up looking like these two pines and how these pines could have possibly grown together?

Mathew explored the possibilities in his head. *There's no way Scott could have tied these trees together when he planted them – they were too small and too far apart to reach each other. William could have come up and somehow joined them together, but why? And even if he had, the real question is how in the world did the image of these trees get into my head as an idea for a sculpture?*

Not willing to give up, Mathew remembered back to the time he originally came up with the idea for the sculpture. *Amanda and I were in Sedona, and we had just finished reading the last part of Scott and Susan's story regarding Friendship Point, with the snake and the rat. And then when we left Sedona and drove back to San Diego, I felt inspired by our time in Sedona and the idea just came to me.* Reliving the drive home, Mathew continued to probe his memories: *But I never saw the pinion pines, and Scott had not yet mentioned them in his story.*

Flustered, Mathew turned to Amanda, "I can't figure it out. I can't figure out how my sculpture and these pinions look so much alike."

Smiling, Amanda gently touched Mathew's cheek and softly said, "Mathew, can you feel the energy in this place? Close your eyes and you can almost feel the presence of Scott and Susan - right here with us. You don't have to figure out why your sculpture looks like these two trees. Just lean back against these warm beautiful sandstone walls, relax, and enjoy our time here." Amanda paused and then slowly added, "I'm feeling so peaceful right now."

Mathew leaned back against the sandstone wall, took in a deep breath and then slowly exhaled. He tried to relax, he tried to feel the peacefulness of the place, but his thoughts ran wild and he kept retuning to the two pinions: *How is it possible that my sculpture looks like these trees?*

An hour later, Amanda quietly said, "I hate to leave this place. I feel so good here. It's like we're in a beautiful dream and the minute we step out of this grotto we'll wake up . . . and I don't want to wake up."

Fidgeting, Mathew retorted, "And I'm having a heck of a hard time figuring out how my sculpture ended up looking like these pines."

Fifteen minutes passed before Amanda suddenly shook herself back to reality, stood up and quickly said in a firm voice, "Come on Mathew. It's starting to get dark and it's a good three hours hike back to our car. We'll be walking in the dark." Gently kicking Mathew in the side of his leg, "I know, I don't want to leave either, but it's time, let's go."

Mathew reluctantly pulled himself to a standing position. Arm in arm Mathew and Amanda stood a few feet away from the two pinion pines. "Let's go," repeated Amanda, pulling Mathew away from the two trees.

Leaving the small alcove and entering the larger sandstone grotto, Amanda immediately turned to the left and proceeded a few steps in that direction before Mathew said, "Where're you going Amanda? I thought you wanted to leave?"

Looking back at Mathew, Amanda said in a voice questioning why Mathew was asking this question, "Yes, it's time to leave and I'm heading for the opening in the sandstone wall."

Shaking his head, Mathew smiled, "The gap is in this direction," as he pointed to the right. "You're going the wrong way; in the opposite direction."

"Oh," replied Amanda, turning as she nonchalantly strolled back to Mathew.

As Amanda walked alongside Mathew, he reached out and embraced her in a tender hug. "Amanda," Mathew said, "Today was extraordinary – reaching the end of Scott and Susan's story, discovering this sandstone grotto, seeing the two pinion pines as one. It's all been so very special." Squeezing a little tighter, Mathew added, "I know this is Scott and Susan's special place, but to me this will always be our *special day.*"

A calmness washed over Mathew and Amanda, a sense of harmony filled their spirits, and a glint of the setting sunlight reflected off Amanda's eyes. Mathew smiled and said, "Amanda, I've always loved your green eyes, they're like little green sunbursts of color."

Amanda, returned the smile, leaned forward and wrapped her arms around Mathew, "I love you," she whispered.

Mathew returned the hug and softly said, "I love you," and then added, "More." And then repeated, "Amanda, I love you more."

Smiling to herself, Amanda asked, "How much more?"

"More than all the stars in the universe."

Amanda in a barely audible voice, "I love you twice that much."

*   *   *

At this exact moment down in Sedona, William, Scott's friend and brother and now a husband, father, and grandfather to many Apache children, sat in a wicker chair on the back porch of his daughter's house watching the sun set over the distant mountains. A stillness came over him and a warm shiver made its way up along his spine. He looked up into the darkening sky as distant memories of his great friend Scott filled his heart. A faraway look covered his face and a slight smile came to his lips. William immediately knew. He knew that Scott his friend, his teacher, his mentor, and brother had become whole, his loneliness was gone. Scott had been reunited with Susan, his other half.

Almost Three Hours After Leaving The Sandstone Grotto

"I'm totally exhausted," said Amanda, "When we left the grotto, I was feeling pretty. . ." Amanda stopped to come up with the right word, "...energized. But it's a long walk back to the car and the darkness makes it feel that much more difficult." Taking in a deep breath, "Mathew, I need to rest. And do we have any water left?"

"It does seem a lot further coming back than it did going in," replied Mathew. "I'm just as tired as you are, but look," Mathew pointed ahead. "Those are the lights of the resort and the trail head where we parked our car is right next to the resort, so it can't be more than ten or fifteen minutes away. I vote we keep going – we'll get there sooner if we don't stop."

Amanda, ignoring Mathew's suggestion, dropped her backpack and slowly lowered herself to the ground. Leaning back against a large boulder, Amanda felt the warmth of the sun coming from the rock's surface. On a tired exhale she said, "W-o-o-o-o that feels so good."

Seeing Amanda sitting on the ground, Mathew sat down next to her and handed her the water bottle. "That's the last of the water, but I'm good until we reach the car - it's all yours."

"Thanks," Amanda said as she eagerly took a few swallows of the warm water. Closing her eyes, Amanda leaned against Mathew's shoulder. "You know," said Amanda, "It's very peaceful out here - the boulder is warming my back, your shoulder is comfortable to rest my head on, and its so-o-o-o quiet."

"Don't forget the full moon," mentioned Mathew.

Looking up, "Oh yeah," replied Amanda.

Ten minutes later, relaxing in silence, Amanda half asleep, said in a low voice, "You know Mathew, do you get the feeling that all of our recent adventures here in Sedona were . . . I don't know . . . maybe . . . somehow . . . meant to be? As if we were meant to find Scott and Susan's story?" After a moment, "I mean, when we were looking to move out of the big city, why did we choose Sedona? There were thousands of other cities to choose from. And of all the houses in Sedona, why were you obsessed over this one? Not only obsessed, but you were consumed for months over this house. You just had to come see it. And once you saw it, we had to purchase it. And . . . what are the odds that you would find the hidden compartment in Scott's old desk that contained the first installment of their story? I mean why would anyone look under an old desk . . . but you did? And now, here we are living in the exact same house that Scott Montgomery lived in. Is that weird? And how is it that you relate to Scott so well and I relate to Susan so well – at times it was as if we were sharing the same thoughts. And how was it that we could actually figure out what all the clues meant – most of the time I had no idea what they were. At times it felt like someone was helping us. How is that even possible? And come to think of it, how is it possible that all the clues were still where Scott had hidden them so many years ago? With all the residential development, and the erosion due to all the winds and flash floods in the area, and with all the tourists exploring the canyons and hills it's a miracle that none of the clues were discovered or destroyed. What are the odds? But the most amazing thing, above all the others, are the two pinon pines in the grotto. How in the world could you have designed a sculpture for a restaurant in La Jolla, California that resembles those two intertwined trees, hundreds of miles away, in a remote grotto in Sedona? You had never seen those trees before. It's impossible, yet somehow, you did it."

Mathew, listening to Amanda, squeezed her in a little closer, tilted his head to the side and kissed the top of her head.

Still leaning against the warm rock and against Mathew's comfortable shoulder, Amanda wrapped her arms around his body and snuggled in tighter.

"What are the odds," Amanda continued, still in a soft low voice. "What are the odds that this big adventure unfolded for us at just the right time, in just the right way, so that we could fully experience it? There is no way this could all be just a big coincidence."

Holding each other close, looking up at the full moon, Amanda and Mathew sat quietly. Eventually, Mathew said, "I have no idea." After a pause, Mathew shaking his head, added, "I have no idea why this has all happened to us. Believe me, I've also thought about it. And I agree, there is no way this has all just been a series of coincidences." After another quiet pause, "You know Amanda, maybe we don't have to understand it. We can just let it be a mystery. The world is full of mysteries, full of things we don't understand . . . and that's okay."

Closing her eyes, Amanda said in a slow drowsy voice, "I guess that's all we can do," as she fell asleep against Mathew.

Mathew resting his head against Amanda's head, closed his eyes and also fell gently asleep.

Ten minutes later, still half asleep, still relaxing in the dark, Mathew suddenly lifted his head and jerked forward, "Did you hear that?"

Responding to Mathew's movement, Amanda also quickly jolted forward. "Hear what?"

"Listen."

Sitting perfectly still, ears on full alert, Mathew and Amanda focused on the brush surrounding their small clearing. "Over there," pointed Mathew. "There's something moving. Listen, you can hear the rustle of the leaves."

Amanda shuffled closer to Mathew, "I think I see it. But it's so dark." Squinting to get a better view, "What is it? It looks like . . .

maybe . . . a small fox or a coyote cub?" said Amanda. Getting a bit concerned, being in the dark, in the open, with a wild animal close by, "Let's get out of here, Mathew."

Before Mathew could respond, the small creature immediately began to move in their direction. A few seconds later the animal was exposed as it moved through a beam of moonlight . . . Amanda and Mathew froze. The animal continued to slowly trot over to where they were sitting, stopped a few feet short, and looked first up into Amanda's eyes and then slightly turned its head and looked up into Mathew's eyes.

Nobody moved.

A few seconds passed in silence before the small animal, who seemed to know exactly what it was doing, jumped up onto Amanda's lap, curled into a ball, buried its nose into its belly fur, placed its left paw over its eyes, and immediately fell asleep.

Amanda and Mathew were in shock. They were speechless. Neither could move a muscle. Their eyes were wide as they stared transfixed down at the little creature on Amanda's lap. They couldn't believe what had just happened. They couldn't believe what they were looking at. There sleeping on Amanda's lap, perfectly at ease as if it had been there many times before . . . one ear up, one ear down, one black and one white.

THE END

Thank you for taking the time to read our book.

Please see **GRASSROOTS**, on the following page.

GRASSROOTS

Most best sellers are created by publishers with a large list of influential contacts and an even larger budget for advertising and public relations. At the moment, my husband has neither.

If you enjoyed, *Bury Me With The Butterflies,* I have a three favors to ask.

First: Please leave a review on Amazon.
> Step One: Go to www.amazon.com/books. At the top of the page under **SEARCH** enter *Bury Me With The Butterflies.*
> Step Two: Click on *Bury Me With The Butterflies*
> Step Three: Click on **WRITE A CUSTOMER REVIEW** at the bottom.
> A couple words or a full page would be much appreciated.

Second: Please share your thoughts about *Bury Me With The Butterflies* with your friends on Facebook, Instagram, and other social media.

Third: Word of mouth always helps.

Thank you for your assistance in spreading the word about *Bury Me With The Butterflies.*

Susan Stevenson,

Wife of the Author, Scott Stevenson

SCOTT STEVENSON, ever since leaving Cal Poly San Luis Obispo in 1975, has worked as an architect/contractor. When time allows, he retires to his office above the garage and works at creating new stories. He lives with his wife Susan in the small mountain town of Julian, just outside San Diego, California. They share their house with an orange tabby cat that goes by the name of Raymond James.

You can email Scott at: scottstevensonbutterflies@gmail.com

Scott congratulating Susan at the finish line of the Susan G. Komen Three Day Cancer Walk. Susan was diagnosed with breast cancer in 1998 and has been cancer free ever since.

Scott and Susan rebuilding their house after the 2003 Cedar Fire - at that time California's largest recorded forest fire.